A DEAD COLD MYSTERY

AN ACE AND A PAIR

BLAKE BANNER

One

THE DOOR WAS OPEN, but I knocked anyway. The captain looked up from her desk. She was one of those women who should have been attractive. She had thick black hair and deep brown eyes, and olive skin that in her midforties looked like it was still in its twenties. She had all the right bits in all the right places, but she was somehow unlovable. Her eyes gave me that "what the hell do you want" look. Then I guess she remembered she'd called me, and gave something that should have been a smile but wasn't. Captain Jennifer Cuevas was all about what should have been.

"John, come in. Take a seat. Close the door, would you?"

I closed the door and sat. She laid her pen very carefully in front of her, like everything would go wrong if it wasn't perfectly aligned.

"How long have you been with the NYPD, John?"

"Twenty-eight years, Jennifer."

She glanced at me. It was okay for her to call me John, but I should call her Captain. I smiled nicely.

"You just turned forty-eight."

"Last November."

She sighed, like it was a shame I'd turned forty-eight in November. "John, don't get me wrong, you are a very highly valued member of this precinct..."

"Thank you, Captain. That's probably because I have the best successful arrest record of any cop at this station." I was still smiling nicely, but she ignored me.

"However, things have changed since you qualified as a detective..." She glanced at a sheet of paper on her desk.

I said, "Twenty-five years ago."

She said, "Thank you, twenty-five years ago. And somehow, and I don't mean this in any critical sense at all, John, you don't seem to have moved forward, kept up with the new technologies and methodologies..."

I raised an eyebrow at her. "What's your point, Captain? I get the right results but in the wrong way?"

"No, John, what I'm saying is that perhaps it's time for you to think about allowing some of the young bloods to move up the ranks. There are some very talented young officers chomping at the bit behind you. And you have, perhaps, already given us your best work."

I frowned. "You want me to take early retirement so that somebody else can have my job?" I shook my head. "Not going to happen. We're not here to offer jobs to college kids we happen to like, Jennifer. We're here to serve and protect the public, and as long as I'm doing a good job, I'm going to keep doing it. When I find myself failing, then I'll stand down." She stared at me hard. "Was there anything else?"

"Yes."

"What?"

She reached behind her and grabbed two boxes of files. She heaved them over and dumped them in front of me. She had to stand then, to be able to see me. I looked up at her. "What's this?"

"We are creating a cold-cases team. In view of your exceptional record, Detective Stone, you will be heading up the team. These here are the cold cases we've accumulated over the last thirty years. I'll leave it up to you how you tackle them, but work your way through them, and close them."

I stared at her for a very long moment. "What about my current cases?"

"They have been reassigned."

"Why?"

"I just explained it to you, Detective." She echoed my words from a little earlier. "Anything else?"

I stood and picked up the boxes. At the door, I stopped. "You said I was heading up a team?"

She'd sat down again and had a smug look all over her face. "Yes. Detective Carmen Dehan will be working with you. I think you two should make a fine team."

Dehan.

I carried the boxes to the detectives' room and dropped them on my desk. I wasn't all that surprised by what had happened. Jennifer had been gunning for me for a couple of years. We had bad chemistry, and to be honest I didn't care enough to make an effort to improve it. I was never good at kissing ass, and I wasn't sure it would help much anyway. In her eyes, I was a dinosaur. The only people she wanted kissing her ass were the "New Bloods."

I was scowling at the boxes and wondering whether a Scotch would make me feel less sour, when Dehan came up and stood looking down at me. We had never exchanged more than couple of grunts and nods, so I shrugged and made a "whatcha gonna do?" face

Dehan was the best-looking cop in the 43rd precinct. She could have been a model. But everybody hated her because her attitude was as ugly as her face and body were beautiful. She was about five seven, built like a goddess with long black hair and black eyes, and had a face as sullen as a Monday morning hangover.

"So what did you do to piss her off?" I said.

She pulled out her chair with her foot and dropped into it, watching me, weighing me. "I forgot to leave my opinions at home."

"They were attached to your attitude and you brought the whole lot in together, huh?"

"Yup." She almost smiled. "What about you?"

"I'm a dinosaur."

I pushed a box across the desk at her. "We'll have to organize this somehow. By gravity, age, impossibility..."

She looked at the box but didn't move. "Thirty years, huh?"

I took a handful and started leafing through them: two female arms found in a lockup; unidentified, naked body found in a refuse sack; severed head, later identified by dental records as...

I paused. The next file down caught my eye. I vaguely remembered it. I threw the stack on the desk and opened the Nelson Hernandez file. It was just ten years old.

"This one always interested me."

She was reading but looked up. "Is it more interesting than Ruby Eldrige, a pimp and heroin dealer who was shot in an alley and had all his money and jewelry stolen?"

"You tell me. Nelson Hernandez, found in a back room in a house in Hunts Point, with four gang members who were also his cousins. They were all sitting around a table where they'd been playing poker. The cards were all dealt. They all had beer or whiskey, and there were bags potato chips and little dishes of peanuts laid out. His four cousins had been shot point-blank with a shotgun, or shotguns. Nelson had also been shot, but he had also been decapitated and castrated, and his head and his balls were in the middle of the table."

I looked up. Her eyebrows had risen, and she was almost smiling. "Ace and a pair."

I did smile. "Yup, the losing hand. Somebody was sending a message. But it gets more interesting. There was no indication that any one of them had tried to defend themselves. They were all armed, but nobody reached for his weapon. And there must have been at least three or four triggermen, because the shots were all fired from directly in front of the victims, across the table. It's hard to visualize."

I stood up and backed up a bit. She watched me as I acted out the scene. I said, "We open the door, and all four of us come in holding shotguns." I made the gesture and tramped like I was four men filing into a room. "'Good evening gentlemen, continue with your game, nothing to be alarmed about!' We troop around the table and take up our positions. And all the while these guys just keep on playing poker." I made a gesture like I was shooting somebody with a shotgun. "Bam! Then we blow them away."

We stared at each other a moment, and I sat down. "There was no money anywhere in the apartment, but they found a substantial stash of various types of narcotic."

"Was the lock forced?"

I checked, shook my head, "Uh-uh. And the key to the apartment was found in Nelson's pocket."

"Weapons?"

"None at the scene, except the unfired weapons of the victims."

She threw the file she'd been reading back in the box and leaned her elbows on the desk. "How about blood from the castration and the beheading?"

I pulled out the ME's report and tossed it to her. She scanned it while I read. After a moment, she said, "Both the castration and the beheading were postmortem. There was minimal bleeding."

"Lead detective was Sam Goodman. Now retired. It was suspected at the time that Nelson and his gang may have run afoul of the Mob, but a total lack of evidence or witnesses meant the case foundered."

"Foundered..."

"Yeah. The other victims were Dickson Rodriguez, Evandro Perez, José Perez, and Geronimo Peralta. All cousins of Nelson's, and Evandro and José were brothers."

We spent the next hour studying the case and looking at the pictures of the crime scene. Eventually I called Sam and asked him if we could drop by to discuss the case with him. He was friendly and said to come right over.

She eyed my car for a moment but didn't comment. I have a right-hand drive burgundy Jaguar Mark II from 1964, with 210 bhp. It is beautiful, elegant, and powerful, the way a car should be.

As we pulled out of the lot, Dehan put on her aviators to look at me and said, "A dinosaur, huh? What does that mean, you carry a magnifying glass and you've memorized six hundred different types of tobacco?"

I shrugged as I turned onto Storey Avenue. "It means I don't kneel at the altar of technology. It means I'd rather see it with my own eyes than through a lens. I'd rather talk to the people involved and get a 'feel' for them than allow the machinery of the system to process them. So if you're talking symbolically, then yeah, I guess I memorize tobacco and carry a magnifying glass in my pocket."

I didn't look, but I like to think she was hiding a smile. I turned left into the concrete desolation of White Plains Road, Babies "R" Us and Kmart, and said, "So, as we're sharing, why the attitude?"

She was quiet all the way to the railway bridge. As we crossed it, she said suddenly and with feeling, "I guess most guys are assholes. I got into the habit of kicking them in the nuts before they open their big mouths." She thought for a moment, then shrugged. "Not just guys—women too. Most people are too damned stupid to be worth the effort."

I turned right onto Morris Park Avenue. It was agreeably green and leafy after the dead concrete of White Plains. I was grinning. "Being pleasant is an effort?"

She turned to face me and smiled for the first time. "Yeah. With most people, yeah."

I took the third left and parked.

Sam's house was tall, narrow, gabled, and green. He opened the door to us like we were his long-lost family. Maybe after forty years on the force, that was how he felt about cops.

"Come on in! I live alone with my cats. My wife died. My kids moved away. I have some coffee on. There are cats everywhere. Come in, sit down."

He ushered us into his sitting room. There was a green sofa, and there were two green chairs. They were all occupied by cats that told us with their faces to sit somewhere else. Sam reproved them and threw them gently on the carpet.

"Sit! Sit!"

We sat. Five minutes later, he sat too, pouring coffee.

"So you're pulling Nelson out of cold storage, huh?" He gave a small laugh and handed Dehan a cup. "I wish you luck. You got a fundamental problem with that case."

He poured again and handed me a cup. "What's that?"

He sipped and sat back, crossing one leg over the other. His face was humorous and intelligent. "To begin with, there was no damn physical evidence. The lock wasn't forced. The damn key was in Nelson's pocket. The place was rich with prints. They mostly belonged to Nelson and his gang. There were a couple of others, on the glasses and bottle, on the little dishes of nuts. But they weren't in any database. There were no weapons. The blade used to castrate and decapitate Nelson was sharp, but whatever it was, it wasn't there. We searched far and wide for four shotguns and a machete or a knife. They never showed up. My guess, they're at the bottom of the river. So, that was the first problem, no physical evidence."

He sipped his coffee again.

"The second problem was worse. Whatever witnesses there might be were never going to talk. Because the background to this killing, and the *style* of the killing, were all saying one thing. Gangland execution. So any witnesses to the killing were either dead or involved, and it's more than their lives are worth to spill the beans."

"Did you have any theories?" Dehan said.

He nodded. "Oh sure. We're talking about the area south of the Bruckner Expressway, Hunts Point. Back then it was a disputed area. The local population were mainly black, white, and Latino. But the drugs and the prostitution were a gold mine for whoever controlled them. Until 2004, that was the Albanians. You know, the Five Families never really had a presence in the Bronx, and the Albanians moved in back in the '60s and '70s and took over. But that pretty much ended when we took them down in 2004."

"I remember. So what happened?" I said.

"Well, that left a vacuum. Don Alvaro Vincenzo, the head of the New Jersey Mob, moved in. It looked like the New York Big Five weren't interested and gave him the green light. So he moved in a few boys to start taking control of the drugs and the prostitution."

"You think they killed Nelson?"

He pulled a face. "Nyeeeah... that was like my best guess. See, Nelson was kind of out of his mind. I think he did too much coke when he was a baby or something." Dehan sniggered and Sam grinned appreciatively at her. "He was a real psychopath, and being Latino, you know, he had a lot of support on the streets, which the Italians haven't got in the Bronx anymore. And Nelson was feeling kind of invincible. But that's always a mistake with the Mob. The word was that Vincenzo sent his top hit man, Morry 'Pro' Levy. Not an Italian, a Jew, but close to the family and a total nut. He was as crazy as Nelson, but he had years of experience *and* the backing of the Jersey

Mob. That was the word on the street. But right there is the second problem I was talking about. Where are your witnesses? Who's gonna tell you, 'Yeah, I saw Pro Levy coming out of Nelson Hernandez's place carrying four shotguns and a meat cleaver'?"

He spread his hands and cocked his head in a "what the hell you gonna do" gesture. Then he smiled. "We canvassed, we knocked on doors, but it was pointless."

Dehan was making notes in a little booklet. I said, "Pro Levy, didn't he turn State's evidence?"

"Yeah, against the Gambino family," Dehan said.

Sam said, "It caused a lot of upset at the time. He's in witness protection now, but word is he kept his ties with the Vincenzo family."

I frowned. "Word from whom?"

He flapped his hands at me. "Ahh! I been out of the business for too long. That was the word on the street back when I retired. Might be bull for all I know. But I do remember that there was talk about Vincenzo having some kind of beef with a cop. It might be totally unrelated, but it was all around the same time and it might be helpful. Don't quote me, right?"

Dehan had looked up from her notes and was staring at him like a panther watching a baby gazelle. "What cop?"

"You're probably too young to remember him, but you'll recall him, John. Mick. You remember Mick?"

"Mick Harragan? Sure, who doesn't remember Mick Harragan? How could you forget that son of a bitch?"

He threw back his head and roared with laughter. He pointed at me and turned to Dehan. "You partnered with this character now?"

"Uh-uh," she said with no particular inflection.

Sam"Don't be fooled. First sight he seems polite, educated, pleasant..." Sam shook his head. "He is the most insolent, outspoken, insubordinate asshole on the whole force!"

He burst out laughing again, and Dehan turned to look at me. "Golly, and I thought that was me."

"So what about Mick?" I said. "He retired..."

I left the words hanging. Sam stopped laughing and said, "Yeah. I think he moved to Florida. Jennifer will know. They were friends. But word was Vincenzo had some kind of beef with him..." He made a long, slow shrug, staring at the floor. "Don't quote me, John, but it's possible—I'm just tossing around ideas here—but it's possible that if you talk to the Feds, they might be able to arrange for you to talk to Pro. Maybe, I don't know. I'm just saying..."

We watched each other for a long moment. I asked him, "You want to toss around a few ideas about whom I might talk to in the Feds?"

He grinned at Dehan. "You gotta love this guy. Who else says 'whom' these days? Whom would you talk to? How the hell should I know? You don't got no contacts in the bureau? Pfff... just off the top of my head, you might try Paul Harrison. I vaguely remember he was involved at the time." He made an impatient face. "But hell, John! That was ten years ago. And I'm getting old. I don't want Feds and the Mob knocking on my door at my age, you know what I'm telling you?"

I nodded. "I hear you, Sam. No worries. I'm sorry you couldn't be more useful. Shame this was such a wasted fucking trip." I smiled at him, and he smiled back. More seriously, I said, "Thanks, Sam. I won't get you involved."

I stood and he showed us out. At the door he said, "Stop by sometime. Have a beer. You won't crack it, but if you do, come tell me about it."

I told him I would, and we left.

Two

I CALLED THE BUREAU from my car. They eventually put me through to Special Agent Paul Harrison.

"What can I do for you, Detective Stone."

"I'd rather discuss it in person, if it's all the same to you, but broadly, it concerns a cold case that might involve the Mob. I figured you could give us some guidance."

He was quiet for a moment. Then, "You asked for me personally, Detective Stone."

"I was told you were indirectly involved in the cold case."

"Mind telling me what the case was?"

"Not at all. I'll tell you all about it, when we meet."

"Who gave you my name?"

"Nelson Hernandez. Is there a reason you don't want to meet, Special Agent Harrison?"

"No, not at all. Can you make it today?"

"I can be there in an hour."

"Okay, call me when you're arriving. I'll meet you downstairs."

I put down the phone and looked at Dehan. "Comments?"

The Jag growled the way only a Jag can, and we pulled out into the traffic.

"Why didn't he do this ten years ago?"

I nodded. "You got any pets, Dehan?"

She stared at me. "Pets? Yeah, I got two rats. They live under the floorboards. I call them Bill and Hillary, and I feed them live Realtors and the occasional journalist."

I laughed. "Boy! Just press any button and you go, huh?"

"What kind of dumb-ass question is that? Do I got pets?"

"Okay. You've got two rats that you feed living Realtors to. What's Sam got?"

She sighed, nodded, and spread her hands. "Yeah, okay. He's got pussycats."

"Lots of them. And they are probably called Mr. Fluffy and Mrs. Cuddles. He was a couple of years from retirement and somebody advised him not to waste his time on a case where there was no material evidence, and above all, the witnesses were too shit scared to come forward."

After a while she said, "Yeah. You're deep. You see that in Mr. Fluffy and Mrs. Cuddles."

"Nah..." I smiled at her. "I just left my anger at home with my attitude. Anger clouds the mind, little grasshopper."

"This the kind of shit that makes you a dinosaur?"

"Yup."

Special Agent Paul Harrison met us in the lobby and led us straight out again onto Broadway. We walked down Duane Street and onto Lafayette, toward Foley Square and the Thomas Paine gardens. He was a big man with slow, deliberate movements and intelligent eyes.

"I am extremely curious, Detectives," he said as we walked, "to know what this is all about and why you think I, in particular, can help you."

"We would like to speak to Morry 'Pro' Levy," I said.

There was a trace of amusement on his face. "I am sure there are a lot of people who feel that way."

We crossed Lafayette, weaving through the cars, and walked toward the gardens. I said to Harrison, "Do I look twenty-two to you?" He eyed me but didn't answer. "'Cause, if I was fresh out of college I'd be about twenty-two, right? How many Feds do you think I've dealt with in the last twenty-eight years? You think I have nothing better to do with my day than waste my time pissing in the wind on Broadway?" He drew breath to answer, but I didn't let him. "Do us both a favor, Harrison, don't insult my intelligence by patronizing me, okay? If I'm here talking to you it's because I have a good reason to think Pro will see me. And if you haven't the intelligence to see that, the only person wasting anybody's time here is you. Have I made myself clear, or do I need to explain any of that?"

We had reached the garden and stopped. He gazed at me a moment through half-closed lids and said, "Have we finished measuring dicks, Detective Stone?"

"You tell me."

"What makes you think Morry Levy will agree to see you?"

We had come to a row of benches, and we sat down. "We're looking into a cold case."

"Nelson Hernandez."

"From information received—please don't ask me from whom—we have reason to believe that Pro Levy might have information and also an interest in seeing the case prosecuted."

His eyes swiveled around the park, like they were threading ideas together. "I'm going to need a little more than that, Detective."

"Okay. We have reason to believe there may be a bent cop involved, and that will have to do. I am not prepared to say any more. If you give that to Pro, I know he'll talk to us."

He looked me straight in the eye. "I am astonished, Detective, that with your background and experience, you would have come here on such a mission. You should know that the witness protection program is categorical in not allowing access to any of its subjects under any conditions whatsoever, whoever you are, without exception. I am going to return to my office now, and I hope you will not attempt to follow me or speak to me. And please never raise this subject with me or any of my colleagues again. Whoever it was suggested this to you was sorely mistaken. Good day."

He got up and strode away, back toward the FBI building, leaving Dehan and me to stare at each other. She said, "What the hell was that?"

"I think we just got our meeting with Pro." I looked at my watch. "Come on, let's get a hot dog."

As we walked, she said, "This is deep."

"Deep is your word du jour."

"Whatever. He's taking a message back to Pro, who is on witness protection but still in with the Vincenzo family, against bureau policy, so that Pro will have a meeting with us because he and the Vincenzos have an interest in finding Mick Harragan?"

"That about sums it up, Dehan."

"We are being used by the Mafia."

"They are *trying* to use us. Whether we let them or not is up to us." We got to the stand and I ordered two hot dogs. I watched her a minute. She looked troubled. "You up for this?"

She nodded. "Oh yeah."

Three

THE CALL CAME AT THREE a.m. I squinted at the screen. It said the number was withheld. When I answered, a deep voice came over the line.

"Stone?"

"Yeah. Who is this? It's three in the morning..."

"You're going to go to LaGuardia. You're going to go to the Fastair desk. You tell 'em who you are. There is a plane gonna take you to see you-know-who."

"You-know-who?"

"Yeah, you know... *you-know-who*. You got that?"

I rubbed my face and sighed. "Yeah, I got it." I hung up, then swung my legs out of bed and thought of Dehan. For a moment I considered not calling her, but changed my mind. I pressed her speed dial.

"What?"

"Get dressed. I'll be there to pick you up in twenty minutes."

"Why?"

"We are going to meet you-know-who."

Dehan had an apartment in an old oxblood block in the Foxhurst district. She was waiting in the doorway when I arrived. She ran down and climbed in.

"Who would have guessed my life would become so glamorous when I teamed up with you, Detective Stone? What's happening?"

I told her what I knew. She thought about it for a bit and said, "So nobody knows where we are, and we don't know where we're going."

"Yup. But we're still naïve enough to trust that the FBI would not set us up."

She gave me the once-over. "What's that, the royal we?"

"We'll take it a step at a time. See where it leads."

There was a pilot waiting for us at the Fastair desk. He led us out onto the tarmac and across to a small jet. As we boarded, I asked him, "Where are we going?"

He looked surprised and smiled.

"You're boarding an air taxi and you don't know where you're going? That's a first for me. I have instructions to fly you to Port Lavaca, on the Matagorda Bay. About twenty miles outside Victoria. Flight time is about three hours, so we should be there at..." He checked his watch. "Thirty minutes after eight." He smiled at us both and added, "Cabin crew will be serving you breakfast shortly after takeoff."

I sat and Dehan sat opposite me across a small table. She said, "I feel like James Bond. Did you bring your tux? Next thing we'll be sipping martinis and assassinating Third World presidents."

I smiled. Dehan had a sense of humor. Who knew? She caught my look and said, "There is a serious side to this, Stone." I nodded. She went on, "The bureau isn't paying for this jet."

"Nope, the Mob is."

"When the Mob lays it on like this, they expect something in return."

"Which begs the question, are the Feds in an uneasy truce with Vincenzo, or is Harrison in bed with them, along with Sam?"

We were taxiing toward the runway, and I knew what was coming next. We stopped and the engines started to scream. She said, "Tell me where you stand."

We began to move, and next thing we were hurtling down the runway and the earth was falling away beneath us. Outside, the eastern horizon was turning a gray blue over the Atlantic, and to the west the billion lights of New York and New Jersey echoed the heavens in their spray of stars.

"I stand where I have always stood," I said. "I live in the house my parents left me. The biggest expense I ever had was bringing the Jag over from England. The opportunities have been there, as they will be for you"—as they were right now, to-day—"but that's not who I am. I don't belong to anybody."

She stared out at the vast ocean with no particular expression. After a while, a pretty hostess brought us scrambled eggs and coffee. Dehan ate hungrily while I sipped the strong black brew.

When she'd finished, she sat back and drained her cup.

"Is that why you never married?"

I smiled at her. "Mind your own goddamn business."

We sat in companionable silence for a while, and I leafed through a magazine. Without looking at her, I asked, "How about you?"

"Same answer."

We touched down at eight twenty. It was just an airfield. It was in the middle of a huge plain that was, in turn, surrounded by flat lands that seemed to go on forever. We taxied to a hangar where we were met by a young guy in Bermuda shorts and a shirt that would have been more at home in Miami. His face would have been more at home in Naples, but that didn't stop him from wearing a Texan hat. He took our bags and led us over to a Jeep Cherokee. He didn't say much, but he was chewing gum and driving at the same time, so maybe he wasn't good at multitasking.

We took a roundabout route across an endless landscape of flat fields to a town called Placedo, where we turned north and drove for about twelve miles in a perfectly straight line until we came to what at first looked like a small town but turned out to be a ranch called Las Salinas. It had a twelve-foot electrified fence, CCTV, and a remote-controlled gate. Our driver stuck his face out the window so they could see it was him, and the gate rolled back.

We followed a driveway for a couple of minutes. On the right I could see eucalyptus groves and palm trees surrounding a tennis court and a swimming pool, a short walk from a large, three-story Spanish villa surrounded by lawns and gardens and shaded by trees.

We pulled up in front of the house next to a Bentley and a Ferrari. A guy in an Italian suit came trotting down the stairs to greet us as we climbed out and slammed the doors.

"Detectives Stone and Dehan. I am Vito." He gave a little bow to Dehan that was supposed to render her defenseless and make her knees turn to Jell-O. Instead she indicated the house with her head and said, "The witness protection program paying for this?"

His smile became frigid. "Morry is out back, by the pool. Would you like to follow me?"

I said, "I'd love to."

Pro was very tall and very thin and had very big hands. He was sitting at a white table under a parasol by a second smaller pool that was built into the terrace at the back of the house. This one was only two hundred and fifty square feet. The other one was the big one. He was wearing floral Bermudas and a shirt with parrots on it. His face was hidden by big black Wayfarers, and he was drinking something large, colorful, and complicated. The thing here was obviously to pretend that instead of hiding in Texas, you were living large in Miami. He didn't get up to greet us because that would have been demeaning to his dignity, but he did smile in a way you could describe as expansive, and gestured to a couple of chairs at his table. When he spoke, his voice was deep and slow.

"Stone, I don't think we ever met. And Detective Dehan, the NYPD is getting easier to look at every day. Sit down. What will you drink? Coffee? This is my morning health drink. It helps to keep my liver clean. It is important to remain healthy." He laughed as we sat. "God knows there are enough people out there who want me dead, without me giving them a hand, huh? What do you say, Stone?"

I smiled and nodded. "Coffee would be great, thanks, Pro. And thank you for seeing us. I know it's not the norm."

"Fuck the norm. We're here to do business, right? Vito, bring some coffee."

Vito left. "Are we?" I said.

"You better believe it, Stone."

I sensed Dehan was about to speak and silenced her with my eyes. I turned back to Pro and said, "Just so there is no misunderstanding and we don't get our wires crossed, let's do it this way. I tell you what I want, then you tell me what you want in exchange."

He stared at me for an uncomfortably long time. Then he said, "You telling me how it goes?"

I nodded. "Yeah." I waited a moment, then sighed. "Pro, I've been here a minute and I'm already getting bored. Let's be clear. If I am here it's because you want something from me. So right now I'm worth more to you alive than dead. Second, if you think I am stupid enough to come down here without covering my ass, you've been living too long among gorillas. If we're not back in New York by tonight, you and your friend Harrison are going to be stitching postal sacks for the next twenty years. So quit trying to intimidate me, and let's get down to business."

Pro chuckled. "It's habit. I can't help it." He turned to Dehan. "I like to see what a man is made of."

She didn't answer him, but I saw something in her look and made a note to keep an eye on her when she was under pressure. She was either going to be the best partner I ever had, or a loose cannon and a fucking liability. Right then my money was on the latter.

I said to Pro, "Who killed Nelson Hernandez?"

"Jeez, Detective! Buy a girl a drink! Give her a kiss. Straight away you got your dick out!"

Vito appeared with a tray and set out the coffee on the table. He poured two cups and left. I said, "Who killed Nelson Hernandez, Pro?"

He looked into vegetable drink and made a long "Tssss..." sound. "I don't know. That kid was getting above himself, know what I mean? We hadn't had the Bronx for a long time. The fucking Albanians had the Bronx. But who the fuck wanted the Bronx anyway, right? Then the Mexicans start moving in. Next thing you got drugs and prostitution going down, and suddenly the Bronx is a desirable property. So we talked to the Families in New York. They said they wasn't interested. So we went in and we started taking control, imposing some order and system..." He creased up his face like it was a disgusting shame what they found there. "You know, it was a fucking mess. Nobody knew what the fuck was going on, who was making what, where it was going. It was a disaster. So we moved in."

"But Nelson didn't want to play ball," Dehan said.

"Nelson was out of his fuckin' mind. We talked to him nice, made him a nice offer that he could live with and we could live with. The little punk says he's gonna think about it. He's gonna *think* about it. He says he has connections with the Ángeles de Satanás, some bunch of fucking bikers tied to the Sureños, and he's got to discuss it with them. So we arrange another meeting. We're gonna pop the motherfucker, you know. We made you a fuckin' offer, you punk. You fuckin' asshole. You think you can say no to the fuckin' Mob?"

His face had gone red, and he had a vein pulsing in his head. He cleared his throat and sank back in his chair.

"Anyway. So it turns out the motherfucker set us up. Instead of us popping him, he ambushes us and takes out three of the boys. Tony, Angelo, and..." He thought for a while, making a round-and-round motion with his finger.

"It doesn't matter," I said. "Go on."

"It fuckin' matters. Frankie. It was Frankie. Anyway, so he ambushes us with superior numbers and kills four of our boys. So—and here we come to the part about what we want."

He finished his drink, placed the glass on the table, and smacked his lips.

"We had a man in the 43rd."

"Mick Harragan," Dehan snapped.

Pro considered her a moment, then said, "Yeah, Mick Harragan. We looked after him, and he looked after us. So we told him to keep an eye on Nelson, watch his movements, and set him up so we could punish the motherfucking punk. So he did. Or he said he did.

"He told us Nelson had a poker night with his cousins. Every week they would get together, have some drinks, and play cards till the early hours. It was in a back room in a house off Randall Avenue in Hunts Point. It was just them. On this particular night they would have a stash of takings from the rackets. He didn't know how much, but it would be several hundred grand. All we had to do was go in and pop 'em."

"So what happened?"

"We got there at two thirty a.m., and the place is crawling with cops. Fuckin' cops everywhere!" He turned to Dehan. "No offense. But there were. There were fucking cops all over the fucking place. Nelson was already dead."

I finished my coffee. It was cold.

Dehan spoke my mind.

"Pro, you've brought us an awful long way to tell us practically nothing. How does this help us, and what do you want from us?"

"I'm coming to that." He held up his hands like he was going to confess to something. "Those were not good times for us. We'd taken some bad knocks from the Feds, we'd lost some territory, there were thousands of fuckin' immigrants coming in taking our business. They were bad times. So the Bronx right then was a vacuum…"

I glanced at Dehan. She'd picked it up too. Sam had used the same expression. Pro went on.

"There were other people interested in moving in on that territory. And one of the gangs that was up and coming at that time was the Chinese Triad. It was a long way from Chinatown, but they figured they could move in and control the action. There were Chinks seen there that night, and they were probably as keen to get rid of Nelson as we were. Why were they there? Why that night? Now…" He paused and took off his shades to look at me. "The one man who *knows* the answer, the one man who knows what happened that night, is Mick Harragan. And what I want, what Mr. Vincenzo wants, is Mick Harragan. Because I am goddamn sure that he set us up the first time, and he sold us out again the second time. And it just so happens that Mick fuckin' Harragan disappeared the night Nelson was killed."

"What do you mean he disappeared? He retired to Florida."

"Did he? Have you tried to contact him there? Let me tell you, Stone, Mick Harragan ain't in Florida. He ain't nowhere. Mick Harragan has disappeared into thin air, along with Nelson's stash." He shrugged and pulled a face. "Maybe it was the Chinks, maybe it was Mick. Either way, we want Mick."

"What do you mean, you want Mick? You think we are going to find him and hand him over to you?"

He looked at me with dead eyes and shook his head. "Just, when you find him, let the relevant authorities know. You understand me?" He grinned. "Just do your job, Detectives, and we will take care of everything else."

Four

WE WERE DRIVEN BACK to the airfield and landed back in LaGuardia by three in the afternoon. We didn't talk much. Dehan was not exactly a chatterbox at the best of times, but on the flight back from Port Lavaca, she was more withdrawn than usual. I gave her her space and snatched a couple of hours' sleep.

It was hot and humid as we crossed the parking lot. I opened the doors of the Jag, and we sat for a while letting it cool down. I pulled out my cell and called my contact at the bureau. We weren't exactly friends, but we'd built up a good professional relationship over the years. I put it on speaker, placed it on the dash, and closed the door, indicating with my head that Dehan should do the same.

"John, how's it going my friend? What can I do for you?"

"Bernie, I have a request. It's a little sensitive and requires some discretion."

"Name it. If I can do it, I will. You know that."

"I need to find a retired NYPD detective. Until now there has been no indication of foul play, but certain facts are emerging in relation to a cold case, and I am beginning to wonder."

"What's his name?"

"Michael Harragan, from the 43rd precinct. Took early retirement about ten years ago."

"No problem, I'll sniff around. You can't check this through your commander or your own files?"

"Like I said, Bernie, it's sensitive."

"Oh..." He was silent for a moment. "Anything we should know about?"

"I don't know yet. But if it starts to look that way, you'll be the first to know."

"I'll get back to you."

I hung up. "I don't need to tell you, not a word to the captain."

Dehan's voice was as tense as a bowstring. "You think he's dead?"

I turned to look at her, but her face didn't tell me a thing. I shook my head. "I don't know what I think right now. But that slippery son of a bitch? I doubt it. My bet is he's living large in Mexico or Brazil on the money he skimmed off the rackets in the Bronx."

"If the Mob haven't found him in ten years, he must be pretty good at covering his tracks. What if the bureau can't help us?"

I nodded that I knew and said, "He had a partner, kind of weak, did what he was told. Loud mouth when Mick was around but kept to himself when he wasn't..."

Dehan spoke in a flat voice. "His name is Jim Kirkpatrick. Everybody called him Kirk."

I stared at the cars in the lot for a long while. Then I put my cell in my pocket and fired up the engine. As I headed toward the Grand Central Parkway, I said, "Don't you think it's time you told me?"

She shrugged and shook her head. "There's nothing to tell, Stone. My dad was Jewish. He was disowned by his family for marrying a Latina. My mom was Mexican. One of his uncles felt bad for him and gave him some money to start a business. So they set up a small café together on Garrison Avenue, near the corner of Faile."

She was quiet for a while, watching the traffic through the window. After a moment, she smiled. It was a nice smile, unmarred by cynicism or sarcasm. "They were nice people, gregarious, outgoing, noisy, fun-loving, totally in love with each other. So they attracted a lot of customers. They made a go of it."

"What happened?"

"I was fourteen. Nelson and his boys came looking for protection. They said Mom was a Latina and she owed them loyalty. My dad told them where to go. They said they'd be back. He called the cops, and Mick Harragan came round with his pal Kirk. He told my dad community relations were a very delicate balance in a neighborhood like the Bronx. That a Jew 'shacking up' with a Christian, and a Catholic at that, was the kind of thing that could upset a lot of people. He said my dad was lucky to be accepted as well as he was, and in order to avoid things getting ugly, the best thing he could do was pay up and keep his mouth shut."

"So you have a personal issue with Mick."

She shook her head. "No. It is what it is. Shit happens, and other inspiring clichés. There will always be sons of bitches like Mick in every profession. I joined the force because one day a good, decent couple like my parents will call the cops for help, and they'll get me instead of that asshole. But I have no personal issue with Mick. He's in the past."

I glanced at her. She was as expressionless as ever. I said, "If there is more to it than that, I need to know."

"So you can take me off the case?"

"No. So I can be aware of it."

"There is no more to it than that. I moved on." Then she added, with a twist of lemon, "I'm good at moving on."

As we stepped into the precinct, she said, "You want me to check the databases for Kirkpatrick?"

I nodded. "Yeah. You hungry?" Neither of us had eaten on the flight. She said she was, and I took a walk down to the deli on the corner. When I got back, she had her ass on the hood of my car. I walked up to her and gave her her sandwich. I said, "You already knew where he lived, didn't you, Carmen?"

She shook her head. "No. It was easy to find. You want to go now, or eat first?"

"I can eat and drive at the same time."

James Kirkpatrick had moved to Northwest Yonkers. He'd obviously had some kind of super pension plan I had never heard of. We took the I-95 and were there in just under a half hour. It was leafy and green in a way that suggested nothing bad ever happened there. You could drink martinis dry every evening without ever getting drunk, and children would always run laughing to school. Maybe that was true in Yonkers. I would never know. I couldn't afford paradise.

He had a gray-blue clapboard house with Dutch gables that looked like something out of one of the darker episodes of *The X-Files*. I parked out front, and the slam of the car doors echoed across the empty, green lawns. A long path crossed his front garden, and we climbed the steps to the porch and rang the bell.

We waited long enough for Dehan to ring the bell a second time. Then we heard steps, and the door opened. He glanced at us and looked at me twice. He narrowed his eyes. "Stone, right? You're from the 43rd. What's up?"

"Hello, Kirk. Can we come in? We need to ask you a few questions."

He hesitated, then kind of rushed his words. "Yeah! No! Sure! Of course, come on in..."

He stood back to allow us to pass. We stepped into a short passage with a coat stand. The passage opened out into a broad living area with wooden floors. Beyond it I could see an open-plan dining room-kitchen area. A flight of stairs on the left led up to the bedrooms and the bathrooms. I glanced back at the coat stand with one coat on it and said, "You live here alone, Kirk?"

"My wife's at her mother's..."

He stood in the hallway, looking at us and chewing his lip. I smiled. "It's been a long time. You going to ask us to sit down?"

He looked at his watch. "It's kinda late. What's this about?"

I didn't answer. We both watched him, waiting. Finally he said, "Yeah, sure. Where are my manners? Sit down, make yourselves comfortable. You want some coffee? A beer?"

I shook my head. "No, Kirk. Sit down. We have some questions for you."

"Sure, whatever."

He sat. Behind him was a bow window with net curtains, and through it I could see the street and my car. It was very still and very quiet. "Where is Mick?"

"Mick?"

I laughed. "You don't remember Mick? He was your partner for fifteen years."

"No! Yeah! Of course I remember Mick! We, we, we were *partners*! Like you said. I was just surprised at you asking me..."

"So where is he?" Dehan said.

He pulled a face. "We lost touch. He went to Miami."

"No, he didn't."

He made like a goldfish and mouthed silently for a few seconds, then blurted, "I thought he did..."

Dehan said, "No, you didn't."

"Look, c'mon, guys! What can I tell you? I thought he went to Miami."

I smiled sweetly and spoke reassuringly. "Okay, don't get your panties in a tangle, Kirk. We need to talk to him, that's all. It's nothing serious, just a few loose ends we need to tie up." He sighed. I smiled at Dehan. "We were just talking to an old pal of yours, weren't we, Carmen? He said to send his regards. He'd love to catch up sometime, real soon." Kirk now looked vaguely sick. "What was his name again?"

Dehan said, "Morry. You remember Morry, don't you, Kirk? He said you and him and Mick were all real close back in the day. But you stopped answering his calls and hurt his feelings." She looked at me, and her smile was kind of chilling. "What do you say, John. Should we call him and arrange a get-together?"

"No! No, listen! Stop!"

I said, "Your memory beginning to work?"

"*No*! What I'm telling you, John! I don't know where he is. I told Vincenzo's people already. I don't know nothing. Mick bailed on me too. Fucking asshole owes me money. I'll tell you what I know, but what I know is nothing."

I sighed. "Okay, let's have that beer. Then tell me the nothing that you know."

He went to the kitchen and came back with three cold beers. He sat and took a swig.

"You gotta understand, until Nelson came along, Mick had the situation in the Bronx under control. Everything was working smoothly. Things had changed since we took down the Albanians, and there was some jockeying for power, but the families in New York had given Vincenzo the go-ahead to move in. It was an old, well-established family. They knew how to do things and keep the peace. You know, firm but fair. The important thing, as Mick saw it, was to keep the Chinese out, because those motherfuckers are crazy, and keep some control over the Mexicans, because those motherfuckers are just as fucking crazy as the fucking Chinese! You know what I'm saying? So Mick was all for having the New Jersey Mob move in. It made sense." He paused and stared at Dehan. "You Mexican?"

"Half," she said tonelessly.

He grinned. "Then I'm half-sorry. No, seriously, I was talking about the gangs, the *Angeles de Satanas*, not *all* Mexicans."

She said, "Shut up, Kirk. Just get on with your goddamn story."

"Okay. So anyhow, suddenly Nelson comes out of nowhere with his *chulos* and they start muscling in on Vincenzo's territory. Next thing he's running hookers and dope. And because he's a local kid, he has the support of the *barrios*. So Pro comes over from Jersey and has a talk to him, warns him. 'Cause you know, Vincenzo and Pro, they are statesmen. They got experience and they are wise. So they don't just blow him away and start a war. They're fair. The guy has put in work—he's built up his business, so all he's got to do is pay a tax."

Dehan was looking at me. Her cheeks were colored, and her eyes were bright. She pointed at Kirk and said, "This motherfucker was a cop?"

I gave my head a very small shake. "You want to wait outside?"

"No."

She caught my unspoken answer, then shut up and sighed. I turned back to Kirk. "Yeah, Vincenzo is a real Thomas Jefferson. So what happened?"

"Nelson was out of his fucking mind. I think he was a goddamn psychopath or a sociopath, or both. Plus he was doing blow like there was no tomorrow, and that was making him more paranoid and crazy. He thought he was God or something. So he tells Pro to go fuck himself. And then he tells Mick the same thing. Mick comes around for his..." He hesitated over the word, then said, "*dues*... you know? His dues, and Nelson tells him to go fuck himself. He don't need Mick no more and he ain't paying him."

"How'd he figure that?"

"He said he'd been talking to the Sureños. They also call themselves the Ángeles de Satanás, like the Hells Angels, only Mexican."

"Yeah, we know."

"Sure you do. The whole Latino population of the Bronx is either in the gang or has family in the gang. So if they got behind Nelson, he was untouchable, know what I'm saying? So he says to Mick that he's talking to the *Ángeles*, and now Mick and Vincenzo got a problem."

Dehan asked, "So he stopped paying Mick."

"Yeah."

"So, he made enemies of just about everybody he could make enemies of."

Kirk looked at her and nodded. "You could say that."

"I don't understand something, Kirk," I said. "Mick had every reason to want Nelson dead. But when Vincenzo asks him to set Nelson up, instead of doing that, he sets Vincenzo up. Twice. Why would he do that?"

Kirk shrugged. "You're asking me, pal. He used me. I ran errands for him. But he never confided in me. He played his cards close to his chest. Maybe he was looking to start a war between rival gangs..."

"Or he wanted to make the hit himself so he could take Nelson's stash," said Dehan.

Kirk nodded. "That's very possible."

I asked, "Where were you the Night Nelson got killed?"

"I was off duty. I was sick. And before you ask, I have no idea where Mick was that night. We didn't socialize."

I drained my beer and stood. I thought for a moment. "What about the Chinese? Did Mick have any contact with the Triads?"

To my surprise, Kirk nodded. "Yeah, sure. They were looking to move in to the Bronx. They wanted Mick to smooth the way. He told them no, it wasn't just the Mob they'd be dealing with—Nelson was getting pretty powerful, and so were the Mexicans."

"There was talk that a Triad hit squad was seen that night. You know anything about that?"

"Like I said, it could be that Mick was trying to start a gang war on Mexican turf."

"Why would he want to do that?" Dehan said.

"So while everyone is pinning Nelson's death on everybody else," I said, "Mick quietly retires with Nelson's money."

Kirk nodded. "It's possible."

"Okay. Make yourself available, Kirk. This is an official investigation. It is in your interest to collaborate. You understand what I'm saying to you?"

He went pale and nodded, then said, "There is one other thing. I can't prove this, but I got the impression Nelson wasn't only pissing off the Mob and the Chinks. I think he pissed off the Sureños too."

"How so?" It was Dehan.

"He was talking out of turn, man. He was making claims about how they was gonna back him up, like his personal army. But I don't think that was true. And I think they was getting pissed at him."

Dehan snorted. "What a dick." She drained her beer, and we left.

Five

WE APPROACHED THE JAGUAR as a small UPS Transit pulled up. While we'd been inside, heavy clouds had moved in from the Atlantic. Dehan was saying, "All roads lead to Mick Harragan."

I nodded and watched the driver climb out of the van with a parcel. He had a barcode reader around his neck, and he made his way across the lawn to Kirk's house. I noticed absently that he looked Chinese. He skipped up the porch steps and rang the bell. "What's this?" I said.

Dehan watched. It was hard to see in the failing light under the shadow of the porch. The door opened and they seemed to talk for a moment. I thought I heard a cough or Kirk clear his throat. Then the UPS guy came down the steps without the packet, looking at his barcode scanner.

I squinted at the house. I wasn't sure. "The damn door is still open..."

There was a bleep. The courier was walking quickly around the hood of his van. Suddenly, Dehan moved like somebody had put a Carolina reaper up her ass. She was as fast and silent as a viper. I scrambled after her and came around the back of the Transit just as he was reaching for the door. Dehan had her weapon in her hands and shouted, "*Freeze*!"

He didn't. He was fast. He jumped and lashed out and knocked the .38 from her hand with a kick. As he landed, he reached for the door again, but she kicked it shut and he turned and made off down the road. She sprinted after him, and I went after her. They were both getting away from me, so I went back and got the Jag, which was faster than both of them.

I hit the gas hard. As I approached, I saw him turn and pull a gun. It had a silencer attached. I felt my heart pound once. I screamed, "*Duck*!" even though nobody could hear me and floored the pedal. He turned the gun on me, took aim, but I was approaching too fast. His gun wavered and he leaped aside.

I slammed on the brakes and jumped out. Dehan was on him as he got to his feet. He delivered a volley of punches and kicks, and I gaped as she blocked and ducked all of them. Then suddenly she rammed her elbow in his face, and he was staggering back. She didn't falter. She was after him. Two pile drivers to his floating ribs and a knee to his face should have laid him out. But he was tough. He fell to the ground and rolled. Then he was on his feet and coming back for more.

One of his punches would have spoiled her looks for life, and I was wincing as he laid into her. She weaved and dodged like a professional boxer. Next thing she looked like she was folding his arms in on each other, so he was blocking himself. She smashed him in the nose, smacked him on his ears with her cupped hands, and kicked him in the nuts for good measure. He was down and out.

I walked up as she knelt on his chest and pulled out her cuffs. I said to him, "What's your name?" She was wrestling to get the cuff on him. He ignored me. "Do you understand that you are under arrest?"

He was still wriggling his arm, and Dehan was beginning to swear under her breath. I went around and grabbed his wrist.

She slipped the cuff on and turned to take his other arm. His hand was up by his mouth, and he was looking sidelong at us. He swallowed. Dehan muttered, "Mother...!" She stood. "Get him up! Make him vomit!"

But it was too late. He was already frothing at the mouth. The last thing he did before he died was to sneer at us and say what sounded like, "*Womeng wefobu zaya landa yinchin tsi shuchen poo shedze hersaw shund atanya!*"

And he died.

I left Dehan to call the local PD and walked back to the house. Kirk was lying sprawled in the doorway with the parcel sitting on his belly. He had a neat hole in his forehead and a big pool of blood and gore as a pillow. I figured the hole in the back of his head was not so neat or small.

We sat on the steps of his porch and waited for the cops to show up. "You handled yourself pretty good back there."

She shrugged. "You want to survive, you have to learn to fight. If you're a girl, you need technique. Brute force and weight ain't going to cut it."

I smiled. "You have a nihilistic, existential, depressing theory for everything?"

"Most things, yeah. I can get pretty intense about steak and fries. Rain. Puddles. The smell of grass. These are all very important things. I'm Jewish. We're intense. I can also be intensely fun."

"I believe you."

I flatter myself most people would have missed the smile she was hiding. I didn't. I saw it.

The cops arrived and we spoke to Detective Stuyvesant. We exchanged numbers and he agreed to send us a copy of the

ME's reports and the crime scene investigators' report. I knew what they'd say, but it pays to be thorough.

As we walked back to my car, the first drops of rain were beginning to fall. A couple of uniforms were setting up a marquee around the Chinese guy. It was growing dark, and the streetlights were starting to come on. We climbed in and I fired her up. I felt suddenly very tired and hungry. I looked at my watch. It was almost six.

I pulled away and said, "Comments, observations, questions..."

"Why did the Triads send a hit man today, of all days, after ten years?"

"Put another way, how did they know we were coming?" I frowned. "Carmen, did you get his address from an official database?"

"No." I glanced at her. "Like Mick, he wasn't on any official database."

"How did you get it?"

"Don't ask me, John, because I am not going to tell you. Not today. Maybe some other day. It wasn't illegal."

"That's good enough for me. For now."

"So the Triads followed us here to kill Kirk. Why not abduct him and torture him to find out where Mick is?"

"Because they already knew that he didn't know."

She frowned. "They were listening to us?"

I shook my head. "Whoever told them we were coming also knew that Kirk had no information about Mick's whereabouts. The Triads just wanted their revenge. At least it confirms the theory that Mick had agreed to set Nelson up for the Triads as well as the Mob."

"How can you be so sure it was a revenge killing?"

I said blandly, "His dying words, roughly, 'We will have vengeance on the Irish penis whose ancestors were not human and also were born from big eggs.' As last words go, they have a certain je ne sais quoi."

She shook her head and sat a while staring out of the window at the darkness of the vast river. Eventually she said, "You're shitting me, right?"

"Am I incredulous because you can do Wing Chun? I developed an interest in the I Ching as a youth and decided it would be better to read it in the original Mandarin. So I studied Chinese."

"The Irish Penis? Whose parents were not human...?"

"And also were born from big eggs. That's pretty offensive."

Suddenly she was laughing out loud, leaning back in her seat and wiping her eyes. It was a good thing to see. It made me smile.

Acting on an impulse, I turned left onto Ashburn Avenue and headed toward Southeast Yonkers. There was a huge shopping mall out there with a Longhorn steakhouse. And right then I was in need of a steak and a beer.

It was dark and raining heavily by the time we arrived. There were only a few cars in the lot, reflecting wet light and making the place look desolate. I parked right outside, and we sprinted for the door. The place was practically empty. We sat by the window and ordered a couple of Outlaw Ribeyes and a couple of beers.

She spoke suddenly.

"It doesn't follow absolutely categorically, but it is a probability that if the Triads want to kill Mick, it's because they did *not* kill Nelson. Because the *reason* they want to kill Mick is because he did *not* facilitate the hit on Nelson, as he had promised to do."

"That makes sense. So what we're saying is that right now our prime suspect is Mick?"

Our orders arrived with the beers, and we were both silent while we cut into the steaks and took our first bite. They were tender, succulent, and delicious. She said, "See? This is something I could get intense about." She took another bite and leaned back in her chair. "Mick or the Sureños. But we shouldn't discount the Chinese yet. Or the Mob for that matter. Pro is a subtle son of a bitch, and he could be playing us. And as for the Triads, Mick could have played them and they still managed to kill Nelson. They are very good at what they do."

"Agreed."

We ate in silence for a little longer. Then she asked, "Where do we go from here?"

"Ten years ago the Triad's top hit man was Chen 'Ivories' Zhu. We need to know where he is now. We need to talk to him. We also need to talk to the first responders at the scene that night. Also..." I sank back in my chair. "It's going to be hard going, but we need to talk to Nelson's family, his cousins' families. We need some background. We could be barking entirely up the wrong tree."

"They won't talk to us."

"We have to try. His mother, his sisters, aunts and uncles. There will be hostility, but these are the people who know the most. Did he have a girlfriend? Did he confide in her? We have to get in there."

She watched me a while. "What about the captain, Stone? She's supposed to be a friend of Mick's."

I didn't say anything. I just shook my head.

The rain had eased. We made our way out to the car through the dark drizzle, over the liquid light of the puddles. Half an hour later, I dropped her at her apartment. Before she got out, I said, "In the morning I'll try to track down Chen Zhu. You draw up a list of Nelson's immediate family."

She gave a funny smile and said, "You got it, partner."

Six

NOT MUCH HAPPENED THE next day. Dehan was busy compiling a list of Nelson's family and close friends, and I found out that Chen Zhu was doing twenty to life in Attica. I made the call to arrange to visit him in a couple of days and then sat chewing my lip and thinking about some gossip I'd heard from some of the guys a few years back.

Dehan joined me at lunchtime and dropped into the chair opposite.

"I got a list. It's pretty comprehensive. His mother. His dad was killed in a drive-by when he was a baby. He was pretty much raised by two uncles and his mom. The uncles were both in a local gang affiliated to the *Ángeles*. His male cousins, all sons of the two uncles, were the ones who were killed that night. Mother has two sisters, both married but with daughters or baby sons."

"How did you get this?"

"I said I was a reporter for the *Voz de Chihuahua*, a Marxist paper reporting on how Latinos are exploited and denigrated in the imperialist USA."

I nodded. "I could never do that."

"Look at you. You're an Anglo-Saxon. You have gringo written all over you."

"No, I mean my conscience would not allow me."

"Yeah? I used to have one of them. It got mugged."

"Girlfriends?"

"There was talk of a wife. Others said a girlfriend. Others said it was several girlfriends. Either way they seem to have been *putillas* and just passing through. There was also talk that he kept Mick supplied with young Latina girls. It seems he had a liking for them."

"That's good. In fact it is so good I am going to take you out tonight."

"Dancing?"

"Why not. First we'll have some dinner, and then we'll go dancing."

"Why do I get the feeling this is a stakeout?"

I laughed and pointed at her. "You are *good!* You are *very* good!"

We were at the corner of Central Park West and Ninety-Seventh. It was eleven thirty at night, and the dim light from the streetlights was mottled and filtered through the leaves of the plane trees. Or maybe they were chestnuts. We were a short way from the Crenshaw Church. It had a sinister, gothic look silhouetted against the burnt-orange glow of the clouds. An occasional raindrop would splat liquid amber light on the windshield. There was something sudden yet indecisive about it, like a drunk who makes up his mind to leave and then falls asleep at the bar.

The wipers squeaked and removed the latest drop.

To our right was a private parking lot fringed by gardens that formed a kind of courtyard outside the apartment block we were watching. It was still and quiet. Dehan had her window open a few inches.

"This is a pretty long shot, Stone."

"You saw what the guy in Yonkers was prepared to do. If we're going to get Zhu to open up, we need more than a smile and 'please.'"

"What if he doesn't show?"

"If what I was told is true, he'll show."

"How—"

I cut her off. "How reliable? Pretty reliable. If I didn't think it was worth it, we wouldn't be here."

She eyed me curiously. "I guess that's true at that."

Voices made her turn and look. They were men's voices, young, laughing, speaking Chinese. They came walking along a concrete pathway among the trees, from the entrance to the block. Their clothes had the vulgar elegance of Italian designers. A Lexus parked across from us flashed and bleeped as they approached it. They stepped into the glow of a streetlight, and I recognized one of them as Zak Zhu, Chen's younger brother. They all climbed into the car and took off. I let them get ahead of us a way and followed. I had a pretty good idea where they were going, so I could afford to give them space.

They turned right onto West Ninety-Seventh and then left at the end of the block onto Columbus. I settled back and said, "If I'm right, it'll now be a straight line all the way to West Fifth-Second."

I was. We cruised for five or ten minutes along Columbus and onto Ninth. On Ninth I turned right into West Fifty-Third and parked. Then we walked through the drizzle to West Fifty-Second and found the Therapy Bar, a well-known gay nightclub. I'd been told it was a regular hangout for him and, as I'd expected, he was there. The Lexus was parked with its hazards flashing, and he was leaning in through the driver's window. I figured his friend was going to find somewhere to park. I smiled at Dehan and said, "Come on, darling, let me get a picture of you."

She struck a pose, and I took a picture of Zak.

It was midweek, so it wasn't very crowded, and we pushed inside. Red and blue flashing lights made the visibility poor, but I figured it would be good enough. We made our way to the bar and ordered two beers. I stood with my back to the door, and Dehan kept a watch on who came in. The thumping was so loud, conversation and thought were practically impossible. But this wasn't a place you came to think or talk. After a moment, she leaned into me and said, "He's just come in."

I threw back my head and laughed like she'd said something hilarious. She laughed too and picked up her cell. I struck a pose, and she took another picture of Zak. I turned and surveyed the scene. Zak and his pals were sitting at a corner table. Since they'd walked through the door, their gestures and mannerisms had become exaggerated. They managed to be more effeminate than any woman I had ever seen. They left their things at the table and ran with little steps to the dance floor. Zak was wearing torn jeans and a string vest, which he removed while he danced. After that he and his friends proceeded to display their sexual proclivities in an unequivocal and unabashed fashion, while Dehan and I made a video record of their unrestrained social statements.

So far the evening had gone without a hitch, exactly as I had hoped. It was as I was paying and we were about to head for the door that things started to turn problematic. I noticed a large presence at my elbow. I looked and the guy must have been six foot seven if he was an inch. He had a bald head and a Freddy Mercury moustache. To complete the stereotype, he had chosen a T-shirt with black-and-white horizontal stripes. His voice was big enough to drown out the thumping of the music. Oddly, his accent was South African.

"You bin filming a lot, mate."

I gave him a friendly grin and said, "Yuh, ve are from Norvey. Ve loff de crazy New York scene." I held out my hand. "I am Rune, and zis is my vife, Inga."

His face said he thought I was a clown and not a very funny one. He ignored my hand and nodded at my cell. "All your pictures and movies are of the sem guy."

"Yuh! He is *vild*, yuh?"

"Your exent is not Norwegian... Who are you? Why are you stalking Zek?"

I nodded vigorously like I hadn't heard him, but I was being polite, and I took Dehan's hand in mine and began to push past him.

"Yah, yah! Vee moost goink now!"

He put a hand like a small cow on my chest and said, "Why heff you bin filming Zek?"

Dehan came in real close to him and crooked her finger. He bent down to listen to her, and I saw his eyes bulge. I heard her shout in his ear. "Zis is fot vee are callingk zee Norwegian nut cruncher. Sit down unt drinking zee visky or vee are blowingk you fuckingk head off. Vee are makingk ourselves understood, yuh?"

I smiled at the barkeep while Dehan eased our Seth Efrikan friend onto a stool. I pointed at him, mouthed, "Double Scotch," and showed with my fingers it should be a big one. I put ten bucks on the bar. Least I could do was pay for his drink.

We moved toward the door while the Veldt Wonder wept into his whiskey. As we pushed out, we heard a shout and made off at a run toward Ninth Avenue. I glanced back as we dodged through the traffic and saw a small plume of angry, half-dressed young men explode into the street.

We made it to Fifty-Third and climbed into my car. Nobody was following us, but I didn't waste time. I fired up the engine and turned onto Tenth Avenue, and headed north toward the Bronx and the 43rd precinct.

"I'm going to download the pictures onto my laptop and print them," I said. "You want me to drop you at your apartment?"

She shrugged. "I could crash on your couch and we could make an early start in the morning."

I didn't answer for a moment, like her suggestion was inconvenient for some reason. I bit back the smile and said, "I can let you have a bedroom. If you promise not to make the sheets dirty, I can let you have a bed too."

She looked out of the window, away from me. The rain had suddenly grown heavy, and the wipers were squeaking a sleepy rhythm. Red, amber, and green lights splashed in squalls across the windshield. She said, "Whatever."

Seven

MY APPOINTMENT WITH Chen Zhu was at one in the afternoon. It was a five- or six-hour drive, so we got four hours' sleep and were up and out by six a.m. Attica the prison is just outside Attica the town, and about the same size. It's about a mile in length and about a quarter of a mile across at its widest point. There is a strange, eerie feel about the place, like it belongs in one of those late '60s dystopian sci-fi movies, where the setting and the system are idyllic, it's just the people that are wrong.

We parked in the lot, and fifteen minutes later we were sitting in a secure room, waiting for Chen Zhu to be shown in. There was a loud buzz and a clang. The door opened and two guards led in a man who, even chained hand and foot, was terrifying to behold.

It wasn't just his size, though he was tall, muscular, and agile. It was his face, the complete absence of expression and the deadness of his eyes. They communicated just one thing: he could watch an unlimited amount of suffering and feel absolutely nothing.

He was placed in the chair opposite us, and his wrists were cuffed to the table. The guards told us they would be just outside and left us alone. He watched me a moment. He didn't blink. Then he watched Dehan in the same way. After that he settled down to watching the wall behind us.

"Zhu, I am Detective Stone, and this is my partner, Detective Dehan. We need to ask you some questions about the murder ten years ago of Nelson Hernandez in the Bronx. I know you're in for twenty to life. If you help us, that will help you, in the long run, to get parole. Are you willing to answer our questions?"

I got exactly the response I had expected. Nothing at all. I was pretty sure he had put himself into a trance. Dehan said, "You have nothing to lose, Zhu. No one is going to accuse you of a loss of honor or a loss of face. All we want is for you to fill in a few details on a cold case."

Same response. I asked him, "Did you kill Nelson Hernandez ten years ago in the Bronx?"

He blinked, but it was probably just his time for blinking that month. It didn't tell me anything. Dehan looked at me like she was wondering why I was taking so long. I was wondering myself. I guess I just didn't like doing it, but Carmen was done waiting. She said, "Do you see much of your brother Zak? He ever come and visit you?" His gaze shifted from the wall to Dehan's eyes. She went on, "He's kinda the black sheep of the family, huh?"

I said, "Actually we bumped into him and some of his friends last night." His eyes shifted to me, but all I could read there was that somehow, some day, he intended to kill us. I said, "Does the family know?" I gave a small laugh and spread my hands. "This is New York, in the new millennium. What's a bit of homosexuality in the family? No big deal, right?"

His face went rigid, and all the color drained out of it. This was true rage, and unleashed it must have been a truly terrifying sight. I was glad he was chained. I stared him in the eye and said, "Oh, they don't know?"

Dehan said, "You're kidding me. Your grandfather, the head of the most powerful Triad gang in the eastern United States, does not know that his grandson is gay?" She looked at me, then back at him. "Well, what do you think would happen, Zhu, if he found out? I mean, I know that family is really important to you, and I think that a life choice as profound as this one is something he should share with the family, don't you?"

I reached in my pocket and pulled out a large envelope. His gaze followed it onto the table. I shook out the photographs and spread them out in front of him. He turned away. I went on, "And I would say he was pretty committed to his life choice, wouldn't you, Detective Dehan?"

She reached down and pulled my laptop out of her shoulder bag. She opened it up, hit Play, and spun it round for him to see the screen. I could hear the thumping and thudding of the music from the night before, and the shouts and screams. He refused to look. "You ought to have a look, Zhu. Because if you don't start talking to me, the next people to see this will be your father and your grandfather."

He spoke for the first time. I was surprised he had no accent.

"Turn it off. Take the pictures away."

I left it playing. "Are you going to talk to us?"

He nodded. I turned the laptop around and turned it off, then collected up the pictures. "Did you kill Nelson Hernandez?"

He shook his head. "No."

"What happened that night?"

"Mick Harragan contacted us couple of weeks before. He said there was an opportunity for us to move in to Hunts Point. Till then our policy had been to stay around Chinatown in Manhattan. But things were changing, and some of the younger men favored the idea of expanding out. There was a growing Asian population in the Bronx. Mick said the Mafia weren't interested, and all we had to contend with was the Mexicans. He said the Mexicans were not organized, and with our resources we could control them. There was a lot of money to be made in prostitution and drugs. Prostitution and drugs is what we do."

Dehan said, "But he told you there was just one obstacle."

Zhu nodded. "Nelson Hernandez. He said if we could take out Nelson, we would own the neighborhood. He wanted a fee for information on where and when to hit Nelson, and he wanted a retainer every month."

I asked him, "How much?"

"Twenty-five K for the information, and twenty-five K a month."

Dehan asked, "So that was fifty K upfront?"

"Yeah. When we got there, Nelson was dead. His head and his balls were on the table. There were four other guys dead too. It was an execution. We had a man outside, watching, who told us the cops were coming. We got out just in time, otherwise we would've gone down for it. Mick set us up and walked away with fifty grand."

Dehan shook her head. "Why would he do that?"

He turned his direct stare on her. "That isn't complicated. He knew his time was up. He was approaching retirement. Every year the system was getting harder to play. Every year there was a new bunch of clean cops coming onto the force, and every year it was getting harder for him to hold on to his position. He was beginning to feel the heat. It was just a matter of time before somebody took him down, either to clean up the show or to replace him. So he played us, Nelson and the Italians against each other. He took fifty grand from us. I don't know how much he took from the Italians, but at least that much, and what he took from Nelson must have been close to five hundred K. Plus, whatever he'd been stashing away for the last couple of years, I figure he ran with a couple of million at least. Maybe five."

I said, "So while you're looking at the Mob, the Mob are looking at you, and the cops are looking at you both. Nobody is looking at Mick, who quietly slips away."

"That's how I figure it."

Dehan asked, "So where'd he go?"

I was expecting the same answer I'd got from everybody, so it was a surprise when he answered without hesitation, "Mexico."

"Mexico? How does that make sense? He just killed five guys who are in with the Sureños and he goes to Mexico?"

He smiled and shook his head. It was the most expressive thing I'd seen him do. "You think on the surface. You got to ask deeper questions. Ask yourself, how much would the Sureños pay Mick Harragan to kill Nelson?"

I dropped back in my chair and stared at him. "He was a fucking embarrassment to them. Mick wasn't causing the turf war, he was *playing* the turf war the *Nelson* was creating."

"The Sureños wanted Nelson out of the way more than anybody. With Nelson gone, they hoped we'd go back to Chinatown and they could negotiate a deal with the Jersey Mob. They knew Mick had a beef with Nelson because Nelson had stopped paying him. Mick wanted to make a stash and get out. So he struck a deal: he kills Nelson, they pay him and give him a safe place to retire. Ask yourself, which is the one group that isn't chasing after Mick?"

"The very group you'd expect to be out for vengeance and punishment," said Dehan.

I said, "You know this? You got proof?"

He shook his head but then said, "When we came out of Nelson's place, we saw the Italians there. They thought we'd killed Nelson, so we knew they didn't do it. We went and looked for Mick. His house was empty, but there was a bottle of tequila in the breakfast bar in the kitchen, with two glasses. We searched the place. There was nothing, but we found brochures."

"Mexico?"

"Nelson had a couple of bitches. Mick has a thing for Mexican girls. Nelson kept him supplied. I figure Mexico is where he went, with one of the bitches."

We sat in silence for a moment. Dehan said, "We done?" I nodded. She picked up the laptop and the pictures and showed them to Zhu. "Send your brother to college. Get him out of the rackets. Give him a chance to become the human being you never did. You obviously love him, so do the right thing by him. If I see him going into the family business, Zhu, this goes to your grandfather."

He stared at her but didn't answer, and we left.

In the lot, she leaned on the roof of the Jag and stared at the woodlands that surrounded us.

"You buy it?"

I leaned on the other side. A rook laughed at us without much commitment.

"Do I buy it? There's no hard evidence for anything right now. All we've got is theories. It's the best theory I've heard so far. It has a smell about it of being the right track. But does it make me want to snap my fingers and say 'Aha!'? No. It doesn't. How about you?"

She gave me a small smile that unsettled me for some reason. "What you said."

She got in and we drove to Attica to eat pizza.

Eight

I CHEWED ON THE LAST piece of crust. I was looking out of the window, but in my mind I was seeing the five men sitting around a table, drinking beer and whiskey, eating crisps and nuts, playing poker.

Dehan said, "They're sitting at the table." She was tipping a glass of sparkling water this way and that, watching the bubbles, "There's a knock at the door. Nobody gets up, but somebody opens it."

"The same person who left their prints on the glasses and the dishes of nuts."

"Right. She opens the door and they come in fast. It's like a raid. Mick's at the front. Who's he got with him? A couple of Sureños. They rush in. They're shouting and hollering, 'Freeze! Nobody move!'—that kind of stuff."

"That's why nobody reached for his piece."

"That's right. They're surrounded. They're taken by surprise. Plus, they can see it's Mick and some guys they know. They're wondering, 'What the hell? What's going on?'"

"And they execute them."

"But the Sureños got to make a point. They're punishing this guy. You don't presume to tell the Sureños who they do and don't support. So they cut off his balls and his head. Leave them on the table as a message to anybody else who wants to declare himself king of the Bronx."

I nodded. "Now the guys leave, and Mick takes his dues, all the money Nelson had at the house..."

I looked at her, and she looked at me. She shrugged. "It sounds awful generous coming from the Sureños, but maybe Mick was holding something over them."

"Yeah... I'm wondering what it is exactly Mick has done for them. Okay, he was there and he shot at least one of Nelson's gang, but in this scenario, he's just come along with the Sureños. It's the Sureños who made the hit. They didn't need Mick."

She sighed. "Okay, then it was hired muscle. Couple of guys he paid to do the job with him. Either way, they leave. He takes the money and the girl. They have tequila. They get in the car and they go, leaving Pro, Vincenzo, Chen Zhu, and the NYPD all scratching their heads."

I played a short tattoo on the table with my fingers. "It's a scenario. It leaves a lot of unanswered questions. But it gives us one thing."

"The girl."

"Yup. Chances are high she was from the neighborhood. Let's pray that for once the stereotype holds true. Latina girls love their mothers. Wherever she is, she may well still be in touch with *Mamita.*"

"How do we find *Mamita?*"

I pointed at her. "You will find her. You will go around the hood putting up flyers, talking to community leaders, talking to parish priests. Did a young girl in her twenties go missing about ten years ago? You will not say, but you will allow them to think, that remains have been found."

"But if she's still in touch with her mom, her mom will know that she's not dead."

I nodded. "Correct, but the chances are that *only* her mom will know, and it will be their secret. So there is every chance that an aunt, a cousin, a sister a brother, a parish priest, will get in touch with us. Maybe they won't, but it's worth a try. I suggest you do it in uniform."

She frowned and sounded skeptical. "You think that will inspire more trust?"

"No, it would just be nice to see you in uniform."

"Take a hike, Stone."

"I'll tell you something else that keeps playing on my mind. How did that hit man out at Yonkers know to follow us?"

She made a face. "There are only two possibilities."

"And one of those possibilities is in bed with the Triads and wanted Kirk dead."

We spent the next day canvassing from East Bay Avenue to Lafayette in Hunts Point. Dehan did most of the legwork because most of the people we needed to talk to would refuse to talk to me. Dehan was half-Mexican, looked Mexican, and grew up in the neighborhood. If anybody had a chance of getting through, it was her.

I focused on the Seventh Day Adventist Church, the African Methodist Church, and the Corpus Christi Monastery of nuns. The priests at the first two were very understanding and promised to spread the word and encourage anybody who remembered anything to come forward, even if it was through them, rather than directly. The mother superior at the monastery had been there for thirty years, and she remembered something.

We sat in her office overlooking the small woodland that was part of the grounds, and she peered at me over the top of her reading glasses.

"This is Hunts Point, Detective Stone. Young Latina girls go missing every year. Some are murdered, others die of drug overdoses, others escape to try and make a new life for themselves. You are interested in one particular girl who disappeared ten years ago..."

It wasn't a question, but she made it sound like one. I haven't got a lot of patience, but I mustered what little I have and smiled.

"Mother Superior, we could get into a long, involved discussion about the complicated social interactions between the NYPD and the residents of Hunts Point, and the socioeconomic and political dynamics that condition those interactions. But that is a discussion which won't lead us anywhere except to where we are right now. The fact is there are dozens of girls, and boys, and men and women and children that we can't do anything to help. But there is one whom maybe we can help."

She gave me a frigid look and then smiled. "I shall consider myself duly told off." She sat back in her black leather armchair and heaved a large sigh. Her eyes kind of glazed, and I could imagine her traveling back in time. "Ten years... 2007... the Indianapolis Colts won the Super Bowl, the Oregon Beavers won the College World Series, George 'dabaya' Bush was in his last year, and the financial crisis had struck." She nodded. "Yes, there was a girl. Maria. She was eighteen or nineteen. She came to me in considerable distress."

"What happened?"

She shrugged. "She wouldn't tell me. She said she was forced to marry a gang member with whom she was not in love. She feared if she said no to him, he would not only hurt her, but also her family and the boy she loved. I tried to advise her that the best thing she could do was to go to the police for help, but she said that was impossible."

"Did she say why it was impossible?"

The mother superior was pensive for a few moments. Finally, she said, "No... but I got the impression that she didn't trust the police."

She gave me a level look, and I said, "Or a particular policeman."

"That could be the case."

"What was her surname, Mother Superior?"

"Garcia. But I am afraid that's all I know about her. She stopped coming to see me. I made discreet inquiries, and the rumor was she had eloped or escaped. But nobody really knew where she was or what had happened to her."

I met Dehan back at the precinct. I was there doing some research of my own when she came in and dropped into her chair. She looked mad, but like she was trying not to be mad. "A lot of girls go missing from Hunts Point over a period of years, without ever being reported."

"I got the same feedback."

"They go into prostitution and die somewhere as a Jane Doe with needle marks in her arm, so nobody ever follows it up because who cares anyway? Or their pimp shoots them, stabs them, chokes them, whatever, and throws them into the Bronx River. Their families and friends never report them missing, because if they do they will end up on a deep-six vacation themselves. Or the lucky ones get out and never write home in case somebody comes looking for them. What the fuck, Stone?" She stared at me. "What the fuck is wrong with this world?"

"People. People are wrong with this world. But we haven't got time right now for existential passion. Tonight we can drink whiskey and ask each other existential questions. Right now I need to know if you got anything useful."

She glanced at my face, then for some reason seemed to study my shirt and my arms. "I don't know right now if you're an asshole or a nice guy. I have a list of six girls who went missing about that time. One of them is Bulgarian, three are Russian, two were local. One of those two was a hooker, like the Bulgarian and the Russians. They are all almost certainly dead."

"The one you're saving till last was called Maria Garcia."

She narrowed her eyes at me. "I decided. You're an asshole. Yeah, she was Maria Garcia. Maybe she still is. I tried to talk to her mother, but she didn't want to know. I left it because she was getting too upset, and I was worried I would draw unwanted attention."

I told her what the mother superior had told me. "That sounds like our girl. How do we play it?"

I thought about it for a few minutes.

"We need to keep pressuring the family. One of three things is true. Either nobody knows where she is, only her mother knows where she is, or the whole family knows. If we keep pressing them, somebody is going to talk—either her to make us go away, or some member of the family for the same reason. If they are protecting Mick—and thus Maria—from the Mob, the Triads and or anybody else who is after him, the last thing they want is the cops drawing attention to them. So if we start pressuring them, one of them is going to talk."

Nine

IT HAPPENED THE NEXT day. We were settling down to some associated research that I had started when the phone rang.

"Stone."

"I got to talk to you. But I can't be seen." The voice was Latino from the Bronx.

"What's it about?"

"My sister. You been askin' questions about girls who gone missing."

"What's your sister's name?"

"Maria."

"Maria Garcia?"

"Yeah. She went missing ten years ago, man."

"What's your name?"

"José."

"Listen to me, José, and do exactly as I say. Be at the corner of Longfellow and Randall in twenty minutes. When I talk to you, take a swing at me. Okay?"

"You gonna *bust me?*"

"You got a better idea? Don't worry. I won't charge you."

I hung up and looked at Dehan. "Let's go, we may have a break."

We approached down Hunts Point Avenue, and he was there on the corner, loitering, whatever that is. He was leaning against a lamppost, and when I pulled over and got out, he spat on the sidewalk.

"You José?"

"Yeah, who the fuck are you?"

"Detective Stone. Turn around. Put your hands against the billboard."

"What the hell for? I ain't done nothin'!"

He took an ineffectual swing at me, and I gave him a push. Dehan got out of the car pulling her piece and walked over. I pushed him again. "Do it."

He began mouthing off about motherfucking pigs, but he walked toward the billboard and put his hands up. I said, "Spread!" and kicked his ankles out so he was splayed. Dehan covered him while I patted him down. I reached in his pocket and pulled out some gum. I showed it to Dehan like it was dope, put it in my pocket, cuffed him, and shoved him toward the car. We put him in the back, and Dehan got in next to him.

Back at the precinct, I took him to an interview room, removed his cuffs, and sat opposite him. Dehan came in with some coffee and some sandwiches. She put them in front of him and sat. He looked at them and then at her.

"What? Do I look hungry?"

"Yeah, and malnourished."

"I ain't hungry. I ate today."

I said, "Tell me about your sister."

He looked at me resentfully. "I ain't a snitch. I'm tellin' you this because nobody else is doin' nothin'."

"I said, I don't give a damn if you're a snitch or not, José. I just want to find your sister."

"She went away ten years ago. I was ten. She was nine years older than me. She was nice. She wasn't like other people round here. She wanted to get out of the hood and do something. She used to talk about going to college. She used to say that me an' her were going to San Francisco. There was a good college there where she could study psychology. She was smart."

Dehan said, "You think she went to San Francisco?"

He shook his head. "She was real pretty. There was a gang back then. They were real tough. The boss of the gang was Nelson. He used to take all the nice-looking chicks. They were his girlfriends, but he'd use them as hookers too. He came one day and said Maria was going to be his wife. She was the best chick in the hood, so she deserved the best guy."

He stopped because he was having trouble holding back the tears. His jaw muscles worked, and he looked away. After a bit, he drank some coffee.

"She cried and she begged him. He said if she didn't come with him willingly, he'd hurt Mamá and me. Maria had a boyfriend from Brooklyn who used to come and visit her. They were makin' plans together. Nelson said he'd kill him if he ever came round again."

"You were ten?" It was Dehan. He nodded. "And you saw all this?"

"He told Mamá we had to be there, so we all knew he was serious. So in the end she married him."

I frowned. "By the church."

"No, man, it was a ceremony of the Ángeles de Satanás. But she was his wife, which meant she belonged to him, like his bike."

"How long did this go on?"

He shrugged. "Couple of months, maybe a bit more."

"Did she confide in you? Did she tell you anything about what went on?"

"She told me she didn't want me to worry about it." He gave a small bitter laugh. "She wanted me to think about getting out, about makin' a good life. But Sam came and visited a couple of times, and he was always phoning her."

Dehan interrupted. "Sam?"

"The guy she was seeing before."

"He came back?"

José smiled. "He was crazy about her. I used to listen to them talk. He said he wasn't scared of Nelson. He was going to save her."

Dehan asked, "Did he say how?"

"It was just talk. He never did. He said he was gonna go to the cops, but she told him not to. She said there was a cop Nelson used to pay with money and girls. He liked Latina girls. Nelson gave him my sister one night, and he fell crazy in love with her."

I said, "Wait. You're telling me this cop fell in love with your sister?"

"Yeah. What? That so hard to believe? What, only white chicks...?"

"Shut up, José. Just answer the question."

"Yeah. He was crazy about her. He was losin' his fockin' head!"

"And this cop's name was...?"

"Mick, they called him Irish Mick. And his pal Kirk, like fockin' *Star Trek*."

The madder he got, the more he exaggerated his accent. Dehan suddenly exploded, "Cut the fucking act, will you! Show your sister some respect! Is this what she wanted for you? Mouthing off at a couple of cops? Nelson kidnaps and rapes your sister, and instead of honoring her and what she wanted, you do your damnedest to be like Nelson!" She leaned across the table and spoke into his astonished face. "It's pronounced fuck, with a *u*. Fucking. Fuck."

I suppressed a laugh and tried to look serious. "So what happened, José?"

"They used to have a poker game regular once a week. Maria and sometimes some other chicks would be there to serve drinks and... *take care* of the guys. One night some guys turned up and wiped out Nelson and his cousins and took Maria with them. That was the last time I saw her. She give me a kiss. She said next day she'd take me to the zoo. I remember that. I'd never been to the zoo. She left and I never saw her again. Word was Irish Mick disappeared that night too, and Captain Kirk."

I sighed, weighing all the angles, trying to fit the pictures together in my head. "You think it's possible she could have planned all this with Mick?"

He shook his head. There was no hesitation. "She hated Mick. She hated him as much as she hated Nelson. Maybe more."

"Did you ever hear from Sam again?"

"No."

I drummed on the table for a bit while my mind did some thinking. Then I said, "José, we're going to find your sister." I pointed at Dehan and then at myself. "We're going to look for her, and we are not going to stop until we find her. You can help. Now you've done this much, why not go the whole ten yards?"

He eyed Dehan cautiously. "What you want me to do?"

"I want you to talk to your mom about Maria. I want you to ask her if she knows where she is. And I want you to persuade her to talk to us. We can fix it so that nobody ever finds out. Will you do that?"

He nodded. "Yeah, I'll do that." He stood. "We done?"

"We're done for now."

He looked at Dehan, and there was a real sincerity about him when he said, "Thanks, Detective."

He left, and I looked at her and shrugged. "I guess it's the way you pronounce *fuck*. Who could resist it?"

Ten

I WAS SITTING AT MY desk with squares of sunlight warped across the old sheets of paper I was looking at. Dehan was talking, but I was only half listening because what I was reading had me totally engrossed.

She was leaning back in her chair with her eyes closed and her fingers laced behind her head. She was saying:

"We know from the mother superior, and from José, that Maria Garcia was an intelligent, sensitive girl with ambitions for herself and for her brother. We know that Nelson decided to take her as a sex slave. We know that Mick fell in love with her, in as much as an animal like that is capable of falling in love. Let's say he became obsessed with her. So much we know and some of it we can maybe prove."

"Mhm..."

"We know that Maria had a boyfriend who, if nothing else, had guts," she went on. "He wanted to save her. Maybe he had a Galahad complex. Maybe he was just a nice guy. We know they stayed in touch even after Nelson forbade it, so the kid's got balls. They've both got balls. So, here's how it plays out..."

"Hm..."

"Nelson has his poker game coming up, and it's a night when he is going to have a lot of cash in the place. Maria knows this. She's desperate to escape, and she's got the guts to do something about it. She has two options: make a plan with her boyfriend, or make a plan with Mick. A third option is do both."

She opened her eyes and stood up, staring out of the window. I glanced at her and carried on reading.

"Sam, her boyfriend, however noble and gutsy he may be, is no match for Nelson and the Sureños—*and* Irish Mick. So, she's smart and she makes a plan with Mick. She makes like she's falling for him too—it's becoming mutual. She tells him about the money, and they plan to wipe out Nelson and escape to Mexico together. Meanwhile, she makes a second plan with Sam. After the showdown, she'll dump Mick in Mexico and come back for Sam and José.

"At the game, she lets Mick in. He comes in with Kirk and two other guys. My money is on two Italians. They blow Nelson away, leave the Bronx open for Vincenzo to move in, because without Mick, the Triads can't operate here. The Italians go back home, and Mick leaves with Maria. Pro makes a big smokescreen, and the killing goes unsolved." She turned to face me. "Maria tries to leave Mick and come back for Sam and José. He ain't having it, and he kills her."

I looked up from the papers I was reading.

"Hm...? That is excellent, Carmen. Really, very good. Let's go."

She sighed and followed me. "Anywhere in particular?"

"Why, naturally, to Brooklyn."

"Naturally."

I took the I-87 toward Randall's Island and the Robert F. Kennedy Bridge. While I drove, I said, "Last couple of days I've been meaning to do some research, but there was always something else more important to do."

"Life's like that." She said it with some asperity, so I ignored her.

"Nelson was killed on November 13, 2007." She looked at me with curiosity. I went on. "We've been working increasingly on the assumption that Mick killed him. So I thought it might be a good idea to find out where Mick was that night."

She sighed. "Oh, shit..."

"Kirk had been off sick for a few days. Remember he said that? So Mick was partnered temporarily with another detective. They were on duty that night. At one in the morning, they were called out to a homicide. While they were on that case, Sam was called out to Nelson's. You couldn't buy a better alibi."

She was silent for a long time. As we crossed the Calvary Cemetery, she wound down her window and let the air beat her about a bit. I liked the idea and did the same. She said, above the buffeting of the air, "It's like a fucking Rubik's Cube."

"It gets better."

She stared at me, biting her lip, and asked, "Where are we going now?"

I smiled. "To Prospect Park, Fourteenth Avenue. To have a chat with the victim's mother."

Twenty minutes later, we stood on her stoop and rang the bell. She opened the door and peered at us curiously. She had gray hair and a string of pearls around her neck. "Can I help you?" she asked.

We showed her our badges. "I wonder if you could spare us a few minutes of your time, Mrs. Bernstein. It won't take long, but we have some questions..."

She stood back, pulling the door open. "Of course, please come in. If I can be of any help."

She led us into an overstuffed living room with photographs covering every available surface. She pointed us at an imitation Louise XIV suite. "Can I get you some coffee?" She made it sound like "caw-fee."

We said she couldn't, and she sat.

"Mrs. Bernstein, I know this must be painful for you, but we have reason to believe that your son's murder ten years ago may be connected to another homicide that occurred that night."

She put her hands to her mouth and spoke from behind her fingers. "My Sam...?"

"We believe he had a girlfriend..."

"Oh yes. She was a lovely girl. I told him not to marry her, but he wouldn't listen. She was a Catholic..." She gestured at me. "I don't know, maybe you're a Catholic and no offence." She turned to Dehan. "I can see you're Jewish and you know what I'm talking about. You're best sticking to your own, but he was in love, so what can you do? It's love. She was also poor."

"What was her name, Mrs. Bernstein?"

"Maria. Catholic name. Lovely girl. Beautiful." She shrugged. "Mexican. Sweet, you know? Real tender."

"Maria Garcia?"

"Like I said, Mexican. They set a date and everything. Then there was some kind of problem. He didn't want to tell me about it. He didn't want to worry me. He was a good boy. You could tell he was going to be a real mensch. He had a pair of balls on him." Again she looked at Dehan. "You know what I'm talking about."

To my surprise, Dehan nodded and there was a warmth in her eyes I hadn't seen before. She said, "What can you tell us about this problem they were having?"

"He was vague, but he said her family were objecting to her seeing him. It's the age-old story. But I had a feeling there was more to it than that. He never told me where she was from, but I got the feeling she was maybe from a rough neighborhood. The way things played out, I wish I had listened to my mother's intuition."

I said, "Can you tell us about the events of that night, and what led up to them?"

She looked a bit distressed and started rubbing her hands with her thumbs, staring at the carpet.

"She broke up with him. He was devastated. She was the love of his life. He was crazy about her. He went nuts. He was crying, he wouldn't eat. He had no father—his father, God bless him, is in heaven—nobody could help him, and nothing would do but getting Maria back. So he went there, he called, he called her mother—he was nothing if not persistent. And eventually she spoke to him."

She threw her hands in the air. "Well...! That was the worst thing that could have happened. Because now he's convinced that she has been kidnapped, or abducted, or being held to ransom... God only knows what he was imagining. Personally, I think she's trying to get him off her back. Her mother has told her, 'you've got to marry a Catholic!' I told him, 'Marry a nice Jewish girl!' But Sam isn't having it. He is convinced that she's being held against her will."

"So what happened?"

"I said, 'Go to the police!' She told him not to. There's a bent cop at the precinct. A likely story! So on the night of the November 13, 2007—I will never forget it so long as I draw breath—without my knowledge, he goes up into the attic and he gets his father's revolver. A very nice pearl handled Colt .45, one of a pair that was given to him by his commanding officer..."

"They sound beautiful," Dehan said. "I'd love to see them later. What happened?"

"So he takes the revolver, and he goes to the Bronx. It seems she had told him there was a man called Nelson who was forcing her to have sex with him and with other men. That night she was being forced to go to a poker party, where she would be raped. Well, poor Sam lost his mind. He was crying his heart out. He was raving. He said he couldn't stand by while the woman he loved was raped. Like I said, he was a real mensch. So he went upstairs, took the gun, and went to look for her."

I frowned. "But he didn't know where to go..."

"He was a mensch, but he was stupid, like his father. He went to the roughest part of the Bronx—Hunts Point, down by the warehouses—and he was going like a crazy man from one bar to another, yelling and shouting, saying he needed to see Nelson Hernandez right then. It seems some feller said he'd take him to him. He led him outside and..."

She folded up, buried her face in her hands, and started to cry. Dehan got up, sat next to her, and put her arms around her. It was like her chest had clenched around her heart and wouldn't let go. Her voice came, squeezed through her pain. "I'll never have him back. Never see him again..."

We eventually soothed her and apologized for having brought back the memories. She called her neighbor to come over, and we left.

Eleven

DEHAN RESTED HER ASS on the hood of my car in the dappled shade of the plane trees. "It wasn't Pro, it wasn't Zhu, and it wasn't Mick. So by the process of elimination, that leaves us only one possibility."

"The Angels of Satan."

"The Sureños, the Ángeles de Satanás. There is nobody else."

"That will not be the main thrust of the DA's case."

She didn't seem to hear. She stared at me, and her eyes were on fire. "It *has* to be Mick!"

I shook my head. "Stop right there, Dehan."

She held up her hands and closed her eyes. "Okay. Okay... I agree."

We started walking, as though one of us had suggested it, but neither of us had, down the avenue toward the park. She kept talking.

"Early hours of Tuesday, November 13, 2007, Mick and Jennifer are *at Hunts Point*, goddamn it! Where Sam has been gunned down, a few streets away from where Nelson has been killed. At the same time, Pro is arriving in the neighborhood with his guys, *for the purpose of killing Nelson*. Zhu is arriving in the neighborhood for the same purpose. They are all there, and they all want the same thing. They all want Nelson dead."

The sign said walk, so we crossed the road and stepped over the wall into the park.

I said, "But while they're playing cards, the bell rings and Maria opens the door to somebody else."

"Professionals, accustomed to killing. They work efficiently. They have a grudge against Nelson, and they take his money, which suggests they feel they have a claim on that money..."

"But..." I stopped and faced her. "They *leave* his stash of dope, of coke, of H, which must have a street value of several hundred grand or more, and they *take* Maria." We walked on a few steps in silence. "And here is another question. Who was Mick drinking tequila with that night?"

She thought for maybe three seconds before saying, "The captain."

"Back then, Detective Cuevas, his partner."

"We know he had a taste for Latina women." We sat on a bench and stared out at the trees and the grass. She exploded suddenly, "That bitch is hiding the motherfucker!"

"Little grasshopper, if the strength of your determination to hit the bull's eye makes you jump up and down and stamp your feet, your aim will become faulty and you will miss the target."

I looked at her. She looked back. "Fuck you. What would you know? You're blind anyway!" She leaned back, raised her face to the sun, and rubbed it with her palms. Then she said, "Okay, Stone, point taken."

I sighed. "But I kind of agree with you. I might express it differently, though."

"How would you express it, Sensei?"

"There is a link between Mick, Maria, and Jennifer that we are not seeing."

"Oh, very good!"

I gave her a withering look that she didn't see because she had her eyes closed and her faced turned up to the sun again. "And we are more likely to find that link by asking focused questions, rather than by making wild statements we cannot substantiate."

"Like?"

"Like, your theory is that the only gunmen we have left are the Sureños..."

She sat up. "Yes. Everybody else was busy. And they had motive, maybe the best motive."

"So we need to find out who the Sureños muscle was back in 2007. Which means we need to go back to putting pressure on José and his mom."

She nodded as though she wasn't really listening.

"Here's another question for you. What would make Jennifer go back with Mick, drink tequila with him in the small hours of the morning, and then go home while he disappears?"

"*That* is a damn good question." I turned to face her. "I'd go so far as to say, answer that, and you answer everything."

Back at the precinct, Dehan set about finding out who were the enforcers for the Sureños back in 2007. Meanwhile I tracked down Mick's address. He had a small rented house on Longfellow Avenue, near Crotana Park. Half an hour on the phone get me the Realtor who let it to him. It turned out he'd only been renting it for a year. Before that he'd had his own house, which he'd sold through the same realtor.

"I know it was a long time ago, but would you have any record of a forwarding address after he left?"

The guy seemed eager to please and said that if he left one, they'd still have it. He went away and came back two minutes later saying that Mick Harragan had not left a forwarding address. In fact, he'd left without letting them know he was going.

I thanked him, hung up, and stepped outside to phone Bernie on my cell.

"John, I was about to call you."

"Before you do, Bernie, do something for me. In 2006, Mick Harragan..."

"The same Mick Harragan..."

"The very same. In 2006, he sold his house. I need to know where the money went."

He was quiet for a moment. "That's a tall order, John."

"Yeah, I know. But it could involve police corruption, the Triads, the New Jersey Mob, and the Sureños, as well as five unsolved murders and a disappearance."

"For real?"

"For real."

"Okay, I'll call in some favors. By the way, there isn't a trace of this guy anywhere."

"I know, Bernie. He seems to have vanished off the face of the Earth."

"Okay, I'll get back to you ASAP."

As I hung up, I heard a piercing whistle. I turned and saw Dehan walking toward me from the precinct entrance. I was surprised at how graceful her walk was. As she came close, she said, "José just called. His mom wants us to go see her."

I frowned. "She wants us to go to her house? Does she know how risky that is for her?"

"I told him that. She says she doesn't care, neither does he." Okay, let's go."

She had a small apartment on the second floor of a run-down house on Manida Street, a few blocks from where Nelson had been shot. There was no elevator, so we climbed the stairs, stepping over kids who were smoking dope and talking about the whores on Lafayette. They went quiet as we passed them, and watched us with predatory eyes. I hammered loud on José's door and shouted, "Open up! Police!"

A pretty woman in her late fifties opened the door holding a tea towel. She looked alarmed. Before she could say anything, I barked at her, "Is José here? Don't lie to me, Mrs. Garcia. Let me in to talk to him and we'll avoid any trouble."

I pushed past her without waiting for an invitation. Dehan stepped in and closed the door.

The woman was shaking her head, saying, "*No hace falta...*"

José was standing in his bedroom doorway, looking sad. "She said it's not necessary to come barging in. She invited you."

I turned to her, sharing José's sadness. "Do you speak English?"

"Yes."

"You don't want a reputation for cooperating with the cops, Mrs. Garcia. It's easier for you if they think I'm bullying you."

She shook her head and said, "And so it goes on? Forever?"

For a moment, I saw in her what other men must have seen in Maria, a goodness, a righteousness that was almost primal, and I understood what they must have felt. I smiled. "Let's just try to avoid anybody else getting hurt."

She sighed and pointed at the small sitting room. We followed her in and sat. "Are you still in contact with Maria?" I asked.

She was shaking her head before I had finished. Her eyes were wise with a wisdom born of pain and patience. She said, "Do you think she is still alive?"

I hadn't expected the question, and I had to think for a moment. Finally, I nodded. "Yes, I think she probably is. I have no reason to think she isn't."

"Then why she never contact us?"

"She may be protecting you."

"From what? Nelson is dead."

I smiled. "Who killed him?"

She heaved a sigh. "*Ay, Dios!*"

Dehan asked her, "Do you know?"

José said, "Tell them, Mamá. Somebody got to stand up to these *hijos de puta.*"

She was screwing the tea towel into a bunch and releasing it again, over and over. She said, "The mothers gossip, we meet, we talk. After Nelson died, Carlitos took over. He was not so crazy. He is very dangerous man, but not like Nelson. The gossip was that Carlitos killed him."

As far as it went, it made sense. "Did Carlitos have any kind of relationship with Maria?"

She frowned and shrugged. "No."

I stared out of the small window at the grim, dilapidated buildings opposite, like a yellow-brick monument of despair. We had found Maria's mother, her brother, and her boyfriend, but we were no closer to finding Nelson's killers than we had been when I put the box on the desk. Maybe that was the way it should be. Maybe his killers should go unpunished.

José was leaning in the doorway. "You want I should talk to Carlitos, see if he'll meet with you?"

"No!" I stared at him. "José, I am serious, whatever you do, you do not talk to Carlitos. You understand me?" He nodded. "If he thinks you've been talking to the cops, you will have big trouble."

"Okay, okay..."

As we picked our way down the stairs, I began to feel mad. We got in the car and slammed the doors. "We pull him in."

"Carlitos?"

"Yeah."

"On what charge?"

"Anything. I don't care. There have to be a thousand things we can charge him with. If he killed Nelson, he knows what happened to Maria."

"He'll call his attorney, plead the fifth, and sit it out."

I sighed. "I know, but we need to get something on him and get him to break."

She danced her head around a bit, like she'd had an idea and wasn't sure if it was a good one. "Maybe Pro could help."

I frowned. "How?"

"Word is that Carlitos and his Sureños are cooperating with the Jersey Mob. So maybe you could have Pro talk to Vincenzo, who talks to Carlitos to persuade him to cooperate with you."

"That's only going to work if Carlitos didn't kill Nelson, and we are inclining to the view he did."

"The other option is to get Vincenzo to supply information so we can raid Carlitos and some of his guys red-handed. We offer him a deal, which includes fessing up to Nelson and telling us what happened to Maria."

I blew out and fired up the engine. "I doubt Vincenzo would go for it. But if we could pull Carlitos in and a couple of his associates, we might be able to play them against each other."

Twelve

BUT THINGS WERE ABOUT to take a different turn. I hadn't expected to hear from Bernie for a couple of days at least, but he called me as we were on our way back to the 43rd. I answered and put it on speaker, then dropped it on the dash.

"Bernie."

"Your instincts were right, as usual, John. But I don't want to talk on the phone. You better come down to the bureau."

"We're on our way."

We took the Willis Avenue Bridge, and pretty soon we were headed south on Park Avenue toward Broadway. We didn't talk. Each of us was lost in our own thoughts. It felt like we were right there, within inches of the answer, but every time we tried to grasp it, all we got was a handful of what we had before. Nothing.

For the second time in a couple of days, I parked at Federal Plaza and stepped inside. We took the elevator to the twenty-third floor, and Bernie came to meet us in the lobby. He was short, overfed, and cheerful. As we walked toward his office, he said, "I got to tell you, John, you have a nose like a god-darn bloodhound. This is going to be messy."

I glanced at Dehan. She was smiling.

We stepped into his office, and he closed the door behind us.

As we sat, he dropped a file on the desk. "This is for you. I didn't want to talk about it on the phone, because we don't know how far this goes."

I picked it up and began to leaf through it. He carried on talking.

"To start with, Michael Harragan sold his house in 2006, for five hundred grand. That's a high price back then. He sold it to a company that turns out to be just a name. It bought the house and has done nothing since. The company belonged to José Guzman. We're looking into it now, but two gets you twenty he works for somebody in the Mexican cartels."

"Or the Sureños," Dehan said.

He nodded at her. "Okay. So the money was paid into an account in Miami. From which it was transferred, twenty-four hours later, to an account in Mexico, in Belize. But the payee account was not Michael Harragan."

I said, "Who was it?"

"It was Michael O'Hannafin. A name change which makes the forging of documents pretty easy for a skilled professional. The chances are extremely high that Harragan is living in Mexico as Michael O'Hannafin."

Dehan said, "That would take it out of our jurisdiction."

He shrugged. "We're not there yet. We're talking to our counterparts in Mexico to see just how much money went into his account, and if there is any trace of O'Hannafin anywhere. But as you know, getting into an account in Belize is very, very difficult. And if he has opened a numbered one, it will be impossible."

"Did you find any trace of him here in the States?"

He shook his head. "When I saw this, we started searching in earnest, going back ten years. He sold his house, gassed up his car, and after that his credit card and his name vanished from the face of the Earth."

Dehan said, "He'd been preparing at least a year in advance. I'd lay money you won't find him in Mexico. He'll have put the money, which is going to be a couple of million or more, into a numbered account, and he will have a second identity. O'Hannafin will vanish, just like Harragan did."

Bernie nodded. "We're going to look, because it's always worth looking. But I would have to agree. Harragan prepared this, and he prepared it well. Chances are, he's in Brazil, banking in Belize." He smiled. "It's what I would do."

We talked a bit more, without making much progress, and Dehan and I eventually stood to leave. But as we were going, the phone rang. He answered it and gestured we should wait. He talked for a bit, made some notes, and asked for the details to be emailed via his secure server. Then he hung up.

"That was Mexico..." He paused and shook his head. "Hold on to your hats. The account has been inactive for ten years. A couple of deposits were made after the house was sold, total of a million bucks. It's been sitting there earning interest. It was never transferred, and it has not been accessed since 2007."

Dehan said, "What the hell does that mean?"

"It means Mick Harragan is probably dead," I said.

She narrowed her eyes at me like her brain hurt. "Who...?"

I nodded. "The same person who drank tequila with him that night."

As we stepped out onto Broadway, she suddenly turned on me and placed her fingertips on my chest. She stared hard into my face and said, "I am going to have an intense moment."

"Really? What are you going to do?"

"I don't know. I need to go out and get drunk! This case is like a fucking maze that keeps going back in on itself!"

I cocked my head and said in a doubtful tone, "Hmm..."

"*Hmmm...*?"

I nodded. "Mhm, hmmm..."

She glared at me. "*Hmmm...*? Seriously?"

"I think we making progress for the first time."

"Explain that to me."

We started walking toward the car.

"We know that Mick had planned to move to Mexico, and there is a good chance he planned to take Maria with him. We can surmise that he got the Triad and the Mob to pay him to eliminate Nelson, and that he paid Carlitos to do it for him at a fraction of the price, while he set himself up with the best possible alibi. He was with another detective at a different crime scene.

"Now, one of two things happen. Carlitos, as part of the deal, is supposed to bring Maria, and the money, to Mick's house. However, Carlitos brings Maria but says he is keeping the money. There is a disagreement, and Carlitos kills Mick and Maria, puts them in the trunk of his own car, and dumps them in the Hudson."

She nodded a lot. "Yeah."

"Or, Carlitos delivers Maria and leaves. But then Jennifer turns up. She and Mick have been making the beast with two backs. Mick has seduced her. Why? Because A, Mick likes Latina girls, and B, because he knows he's been going too long and pretty soon somebody is going to finger him. The up-and-coming detective, the rising star tipped to be the next commander, is Detective Jennifer Cuevas. So he wants to keep her sweet and onside. Trouble is, she's fallen for him big-time. She can *smell* that he is two-timing her. Maybe she watches him, maybe she follows him—who knows? But that night, she turns up while Maria is there, and she kills them both."

"Also very feasible. In both scenarios Maria is dead."

We had arrived and I leaned on the roof of the Jag, frowning at her. "Yeah, at the moment it's looking like Maria's fate is tied to Mick's. But there are two things that trouble me about both these scenarios—*all* the goddamn scenarios. If Carlitos is the hit man, why does he leave several hundred grand worth of drugs at Nelson's apartment?"

"You took the words out of my mouth. And?"

"If Maria hates Mick so much, why does she go along so placidly?"

She shrugged. "That one is less complicated. She's protecting her family."

"If that's true, she must be dead. Because it looks like both Mick and Nelson are dead, so who is she protecting them from?"

I unlocked the car and climbed in. She got in the other side and slammed the door.

"Don't you mean, from whom is she protecting them?"

"Yes, that is precisely what I mean. But nobody likes a smartass, Dehan."

"Hey, just showin' I'm leanin', Sensei. You teachin', me learnin'."

I sighed and started the engine. "So you want to get drunk, huh?"

"Yup."

"Okay."

Thirteen

BUT WE DIDN'T GO AND get drunk, not then, anyhow. As we were cruising up Center Street toward Fourth Avenue, a thought came to me, and I could have kicked myself for not having had it sooner. I said, "Okay, this is a long shot, but hear me out. Here's Mick, a big, brawling, lawless Irishman. A law unto himself. Loves a fight, takes no shit from nobody."

"Long live the stereotype."

"Say what you like, that was Mick."

"Okay."

So in the early hours of November 13, assuming he hasn't been killed by Carlitos or Jennifer, he has four million bucks in the bank, a stash of cash in his trunk, a beautiful young girl on his arm, and he feels like the king of the world."

She frowned. "Interesting."

"He's changed his identity, nobody can trace him, and he is going to drive, not fly, to Mexico. Drive because that way he will be untraceable."

"Okay..."

"As the crow flies, it is one thousand five hundred, maybe two thousand miles by road to the Mexican border. It's going to take him four days at least to get there. How long do you think he lasted before he got drunk? Now, like I said, it's a long shot, but it has to be at least a fifty-fifty chance that if we run his prints, which are on file, through IAFIS, we might get a hit somewhere."

She pulled a face. "Like you say. It's a long shot. It make a lot of assumptions: he got drunk, he got into a brawl, he got arrested, they uploaded his prints but didn't look for a match." She nodded. "It's a long shot, but what have we got to lose? It's feasible. I can see it happening."

I woke up at six thirty with a headache. I was not in bed. I was on the sofa. There was half a bottle of bourbon on the coffee table and an empty packet of Camel cigarettes. I vaguely remembered buying both on the way home, after dropping Dehan at her place. We had not got drunk. I had. Alone. At home.

My cell rang while I was in the shower. I got out, got some aspirin from the cabinet, took two, and called back.

"Detective Stone?"

I recognized the voice. It was José.

"Yeah, what's up?"

"I gotta make this quick. Carlitos has a deal going down tonight, 'bout two o'clock. Down by the Fulton Fish Market, by the river. You go down past the household waste drop-off site, and there's some wasteland down there, by the water. That's where he does his business. He's takin' delivery of twenty kilos of coke. You take him down, you can make him tell you where my sister is, right?"

I felt sick, and it wasn't the hangover. I said, "Okay, José, that's good. You did good. This is very helpful. But now I want you to stay out of this, you hear me? I do not want you or your mom to get involved. When we get Maria back, I want you both safe and sound for her. You understand me?"

"Yeah, okay. But that's good, right? You can use that to make him talk?"

"You bet. Now stay safe."

He hung up.

I called Dehan. She answered with a pillow voice.

"What?" It sounded reproachful.

"You up?"

"No! Go away. What time is it?"

"Seven. Get up. I'll be there in twenty. We have Carlitos."

I heard a grunt. "Good. Okay. I'm up."

She was in the doorway when I arrived, and crossed the road carefully to get in the car. She glanced at me as she closed the door. She looked hungover. She said, "You look awful. How do we have Carlitos?"

I told her about José's call and then explained as I drove.

"We take them down tonight. We separate them. Don't let them talk to each other. We keep it about the drugs bust. Make each one thinks the other is ratting him out. At the right time, when they're getting tired and stressed, we hit them with the murder of Nelson and his *compadres*. They think they're facing drugs charges. When they suddenly see themselves facing murder one, times five, somebody's going to crack and start talking."

She sighed and managed a smile. "Maybe... maybe a break at last."

I needed the captain to authorize the raid and the backup, but when we got there she hadn't arrived yet. So I went to my computer to check if we'd got a hit from IAFIS. We had.

I stared at the screen and sat slowly in my chair.

A minute later, Dehan came in and placed a cup of coffee in front of me. She saw my face and asked, "We got a hit?"

I nodded. "Texas. Drunk and disorderly. Town called Shamrock in Wheeler County. He couldn't resist it, could he?"

She sat. "We have to play this very carefully."

I nodded again.

"At least we now know that Mick was not killed at his house. We can assume Maria wasn't either. Did she go with him to Texas?" I sat back and thought for a while. "We don't touch this for now. First we see what Carlitos and his pals give us in the interrogation. Then we decide what we say to the captain about Shamrock."

She agreed.

The captain came in at nine. We gave her a minute and then went up after her. She looked surprised to see us, glancing from one to the other.

"What can I do for you, Detectives?"

She didn't invite us to sit down. I said, "We have a tip-off about a drugs deal tonight. Twenty kilos of coke. That's a street value of four hundred K. We need authorization to..."

She didn't let me finish.

"I'm sorry, John, back up there a minute, would you? I thought I had made it clear that you were working the cold cases."

I heard Dehan sniff and sensed her staring down at her boots. I said, "Yes, Captain, this is a cold case. The deal relates directly to our investigation."

"You want to explain that to me, John?"

I smiled. She didn't. Dehan bit her lip and stared at the wall. I said, "We're investigating the Nelson Hernandez murder. It's a ten-year-old case."

"Nelson Hernandez...? I thought that case had been closed."

I frowned. "No. It couldn't be closed. It was unresolved."

"I thought Sam had attributed it..."

"It's still open, Captain. But we are pretty sure that the guy who is doing the deal tonight was responsible for the murder."

She looked at me sharply, and her answer was a little too quick. "Really?"

"Yeah. If we bust them tonight and play the interrogation right, we can probably get a conviction on the Nelson case. If we don't get a confession, maybe we can get them to rat each other out."

She was quiet a moment, thinking. Dehan couldn't stop herself. "Is there any reason, Captain, why we can't make the bust? It's twenty K of cocaine, and it could secure a conviction on five unresolved homicides. Am I missing something?"

I saw the captain's jaw clench. She narrowed her eyes and turned to me. "You have your authorization, John, and your backup. Get your partner out of my office before I change my mind."

I turned and shoved Dehan toward the door. "Come on, get out of here." She stepped out and I went to follow.

"John?" I stopped and looked back. "How wide is your investigation?"

I held her eye. I made no secret that I knew she knew. "Not that wide, Jennifer. We've eliminated the Triads and the Jersey Mob. So it's got to be the Sureños, right? Who else is there?"

She nodded. "Right."

"I hope to close the case with Carlitos in the next forty-eight hours." She kind of smiled and stared at her desk. "Is there anything I need to know?"

She shook her head. "No. Good work."

I left and closed the door.

Outside, Dehan was leaning against the wall looking sour. She gave me a glance that challenged me to say something. "Your mouth has two positions, Carmen. Two. Open *and* closed."

She fell into step beside me as we went down the stairs.

"Give me a break! Twenty K of coke and possible closure on five unsolved homicides—and she's going to *think* about it? Like there's a fucking downside?"

"Confucius say, if ritoo glasshopper, no keep big fucking mouth shut, Sensei Stone smack lound head."

"Pff! I'd like to see you try."

"Do or do not, there is no try."

And so saying, I smacked her around the head.

Fourteen

IT WAS DARK. WE WERE on Food Center Drive in Hunts Point, and the streetlights cast a listless amber light over the warehouses and the bare concrete of the road. There was no moon and there were no stars, only a low ceiling of dirty-orange cloud. And silence, the dead silence of the urban desert—the silence of concrete and blacktop. Far off, a ship moaned out of the darkness from another world.

We had four unmarked cars. Two were in the fish market. Two more were parked on Food Center Drive, ready to block each exit. And there was also a patrol boat standing off on the river, keeping out of sight. I'd left my car at the precinct, and we'd used Dehan's Focus. We had a total of eight officers plus me and Carmen, and the guys on the river.

Dehan took the radio.

"Unit one in position. Unit two copy, please."

"Copy. Unit two in position."

She checked on the other three. Everyone was in position. The patrol boat checked too. "All units, radio silence until I give the go."

It was one thirty. We sat without talking for twenty minutes, and then we saw the headlamps in the rearview mirror. The car cruised past slowly. It was a black BMW 6 Series Gran Coupe with tinted windows. The kind of vehicle you'd use if you wanted to let everybody know you were a real bad boy dealing coke. We could just hear the throb of their sound system.

It slowed at the end of the road, and instead of continuing up the west side of the drive, it pulled into Farragut Street, where the fish market was, and disappeared from view. We waited another ten minutes, and a second set of headlamps flooded the car from behind. It was another BMW. This one was a Z4 with the hard top up. It was dark blue and also throbbing. At the end of the drive, like the other, it turned into Farragut and vanished into the shadows, down by the river. I took the radio while Dehan fired up the engine.

"Units three and four close in. No lights till I say."

The cars on Food Center Drive began to move down toward Farragut, slow and quiet. By the river, Carlitos wouldn't see or hear a thing till it was too late. When we were fifty yards away, I said, "Go. All units close in. Go! Go! Go!"

Suddenly the place was alive with lights and squealing rubber. Dehan hit the gas and we entered Farragut doing fifty and our headlamps on full beam, with two units just behind us. Beyond the fish market barrier, two cars came screaming up to cut off any escape through the parking lot. We could see the two BMWs parked side by side. Carlitos was staring at us, shading his eyes. Next to him was Chema, his right-hand man and enforcer. There were two other guys, also shielding their eyes from the glare.

The vehicles had their trunks open, and Carlitos was holding a large package. Chema had another. We screeched to a halt and threw the doors open. I had my weapon in my hands, and I got out taking aim over the door. I bellowed, "*Freeze! You are under arrest! Do not move!*" Within seconds they were surrounded and had ten officers training their guns on them, and a moment later they were floodlit from the river.

It was textbook. I shouted, "*Take out your weapons and lay them on the ground!*"

They were staring at us, with their hands in the air. Carlitos was the first to move. Cautiously he pulled what looked like a Desert Eagle from his waistband, behind his back. He held it up for us to see. Chema did the same. It looked like a Colt .45. Then things started to go wrong. I could see from their faces that the other two were not happy. There was an older guy, maybe in his forties, with a moustache and an Italian suit. His younger companion was also going for the Armani bad-boy look. They both reached in their jackets. I said to Dehan, "They're going to try it. Carlitos must not die."

I was right. Suddenly they were taking aim at the head-lamps, and there was the crack of gunfire. Carlitos and Chema were looking this way and that, unsure what to do. And I was running, screaming, "*Nooo!*" Dehan was right behind me, shouting, "*You take Carlitos!*"

As I ran, I saw everything in slow motion. I saw Carlitos point his Desert Eagle straight at my chest. I saw Chema mouth something and turn his weapon toward Dehan. In my peripheral vision, I saw the back of the moustache man's head explode in a shower of gore. I saw his pal kind of whiplash as he was hit by a volley of bullets. I saw Carlitos's face contract with hatred, and I saw his finger tense. At the same time, I saw Chema's grip tighten on his Colt, and I could see it was leveled at Dehan's heart. I guess my stupidity saved all four of our lives.

I leapt at Chema, cutting across Dehan's path. I seized the barrel of the Colt and levered down savagely. The gun went off, but the bullet struck the blacktop. Next thing my instep connected with his crotch and his eyes bulged with pain. I'd done enough, but a moment of uncontrolled rage made me put a savage right cross through his jaw. He did a wobbly dance and sank to the ground.

Dehan seemed to have read my mind. As I crossed her path and took Chema down, she had dodged behind me and exploded into a scissor kick that sent Carlitos's Desert Eagle spinning into the night air. She had landed in a perfect rider stance and delivered four devastating blows to his floating ribs. He was now vomiting while she cuffed him. The best Chema could do was to keep repeating a high-pitched, "*Heeeee... heeee...*" I had no idea what he was trying to say.

I cuffed him, dragged him to his feet, and pulled him staggering and limping to one of the cars. I handed him over to the officers.

"Take him back to the precinct. Book him. Lock him up. Get the doc to look at him. Keep him isolated. He is not to talk to anyone except you, the doc, and the jailer until I get there. Understood?"

"You got it, Detective."

They put him in the car and drove him away. I saw Dehan stuff Carlitos in the back of the Focus and lock it. She came toward me. I found the sergeant.

"You called the ME and CSI?"

"They're on their way."

Dehan came up beside me. "Let's look at the dope," I said.

I pulled on some surgical gloves and picked up the packages. I guessed twenty kilos was about right. There was a small incision in one of them where I figured Carlitos had been testing it. Dehan took some on her finger, sniffed it, and then tasted it. She nodded. "Gasoline."

I smiled. I had all I needed to start the interrogation. I turned to the sergeant.

"You need me for anything?"

He shook his head. "We got this."

"I'll see you back at the station. Thanks for everything. Good job."

"Sure."

I climbed in the back with Carlitos, and we pulled away. He was wheezing like an asthmatic smoker after a marathon. As we moved up Halleck Street, he said, "Who told you? Who ratted?"

I laughed. "Pal, you've got more leaks than the Titanic. But after today, that is going to be the least of your worries. Today, Carlitos, a whole new chapter of your life begins. Think of it as an opportunity."

I smiled at him. He didn't smile back.

Fifteen

WE PUT CARLITOS AND Chema in separate cells and left them for an hour to wonder what was going on. They were both in a lot of pain, but the doctor had said they were basically okay. After an hour, I had them both brought up to interrogation rooms at the same time so they would see each other being taken in. I then had them both wait another forty-five minutes. Finally I went in to Carlitos and gave him a cup of coffee. The first thing he said made up in predictability for what it lacked in originality.

"I want my lawyer."

"Don't worry, Carlitos, you'll get one. This is one case that is not going to get thrown out because of procedural impropriety. You'll have your lawyer."

"I ain't sayin' a word till he gets here."

"That's just fine. Your pal Chema is doing all your talking for you."

"Bullshit!"

I smiled and shrugged. "Come on, Carlos. What is this, *Alice in Wonderland*? It ain't a question of whether you go down. You both know you're going down. The question here is how hard? If Chema wants to sign a waiver and get his plea in early, I ain't gonna stop him. Let's face it. You're the one I want." I glanced at my watch. "Let's see, four a.m. You'll be getting some kid fresh out of college doing legal aid 'cause he can't get anything else, taking his first trembling steps in criminal law. This'll be quite a coup for him."

I chuckled. He looked worried. "I want *my* lawyer, *Pendejo...*"

"You want *your* lawyer? You want to get him out of bed at four in the morning? To tell him what? That you're going away for the next ten years, can he please get out of bed and come and say goodbye?" I laughed. "Expect to see him around midday. By that time we should have Chema's confession and his deal all signed and wrapped up."

"Fock you! You ain't gonna scare me. *Fock* you!"

"I am reliably informed it's pronounced fuck, with a *u*. Fuck."

The door opened and Dehan leaned in. She was smiling with just a hint of triumph. She gave me the nod, and I went out with her. In the hallway, I said, "How's Chema coming?"

"He's nervous. What about Carlitos?"

"He'll crack in the next half hour. Let's put some pressure on him. Give me five minutes. Then come in and ask if I can help you take a statement."

She smiled and I went back in. I sat opposite him.

"It's hard to get a lawyer at this time of the morning. You should do your drug deals at a more sociable hour." He didn't answer. After a while I asked him, "Were you wearing gloves when you handled those packages? It's good stuff—*gasoline*!" I drummed the table. "Your pal wasn't well up on the law. He thought he was going down for two to five. When my partner explained that with his record of violence he was looking at anything from eight to thirty, I tell you, he turned a whiter shade of pale. But you, you've managed to avoid arrest till now.

You're a smart cookie, right? So you're looking at what, eight, with good behavior out in two or three years..."

The door opened and I turned to look at Dehan. She said, "Boss, can you help take a statement?"

Carlitos said, "This is bullshit..."

Outside, Dehan said, "I think we got them. Chema's sweating so hard he's going to dehydrate."

"Okay. Give them fifteen to sweat, and then we'll hit them with the homicide. You want a coffee?"

She followed me to the machine, and I got two espressos. We held each other's eye for a long moment while we sipped. I said, "What if it wasn't him?"

She shook her head.

Fifteen minutes later, I went back in. Carlitos looked pale and sick.

"Where's my fockin' lawyer, man?"

I looked real serious and sat down. I gave him a moment to assimilate that my expression was telling him something bad. He said, "What the fuck, man?"

"Carlos, did you know Nelson Hernandez?"

He stared at me. "I want my *fockin'* lawyer!"

I watched him. "I have to tell you that we have received information that places you at the scene of his murder, and that of Dickson Rodriguez, Evandro Perez, José Perez, and Geronimo Peralta." I shook my head. "Quintuple, premeditated homicide plus castration and decapitation. Carlos, you go down for this, you are never coming up again."

"What the fuck are you talking about?"

"I can't talk to you unless you sign a waiver, but from what I hear, Chema..."

"What is he saying? What is that mother tellin' you?"

"Well, I hope he's telling us the truth. And I hope your lawyer is worth waiting for."

Dehan opened the door and said, "It's ready."

I stood, and Carlitos said, "Wait!"

I said to Dehan, "Come on in."

I pulled the waiver from my inside pocket and put it in front of him. He read it and signed it. As he wrote, he was shaking his head.

"Okay, I hold my hands up to the deal, man. I'm gonna cooperate and tell you what you want to know. But I did not have *nothin'* to do with Nelson's death."

Dehan sat down. "Bullshit."

"She's the bad cop," I said.

He looked at her, and you knew that was the way he looked at all women. Then he turned back to me.

"You want to know who killed Nelson and his mother-fockin' *primos*? It wasn't me. We was gonna whack him the next fockin' week. He was goin' around talking' about how he was in with the fockin' Ángeles. He married his bitch with a *ceremonia del infierno*. He was challenging the Chinese, the Mob, makin' a fockin' war, tellin' everybody we was gonna back him up. *Su puta madre!* His fockin' mother was gonna back him up!"

Dehan said, "So you killed him."

"You ain't fockin' listening, bitch!"

I said, "Watch your mouth."

"I'm tellin' you. We was gonna whack him the *next week*. Somebody got to him first. Saved us the trouble. Chavez was sending a pro from Mexico. He was gonna do the job clean, go back home, no problem."

I shook my head. "That's not what Chema is telling us." It was true. Chema wasn't telling us a goddamn thing. Carlitos threw his hands in the air. "Then he is fockin' lying, man! Let me ask you a question. How much money went missing from Nelson's place, huh?" I watched him, but I didn't say anything. He went on, "Is okay, you don't gotta answer. Now let me ask you another question. How much coke, H, and dope was left behind, huh? You think, in my hood, I'm gonna shoot fuckin' Nelson and his cousins, and I'm gonna walk away and leave fifteen Ks of coke and two Ks of heroin and ten Ks of weed so the *fockin' cops* can help theirselves to it? *You think I'm that fockin' stupid?*"

I sat staring at him for a moment. He knew he'd made his point, and I knew he knew it. It was the same argument Dehan and I had made to ourselves. But I kept repeating Holmes's principle to myself over and over: "when you eliminate the impossible, whatever is left, no matter how improbable, is the truth." It was improbable, but it was all we had left.

He said, "You want to know who killed Nelson? I'll tell you. Mick fockin' Harragan killed him. And I bet you know that already, but you tryin' to pin it on me to let your pal off the hook. Nelson had stopped payin' him. Nelson told him he was washed-up. He told him no more money, no more coke, no more Latina bitches for him. So he killed him, stole the money, tried to frame the Mob and the Chinks, and left town. You know I'm tellin' the fockin' truth, man."

We left him to stew and went to talk to Chema. He just shook his head and said, "No, man. That was Mick. We was gonna whack him the next week. Chavez was sending a guy out to do it nice. A clean job." Then he laughed like we were stupid. "There was half a million bucks of merchandise in there. You think we was gonna leave that there for you guys?"

I stepped out to the parking lot. The sky was turning a pale blue. I wished I still smoked. When you eliminate the impossible...

I felt a hand on my shoulder. Dehan was standing next to me. "Which one is impossible, and which one is improbable—Mick did it, or Carlitos did it?"

She sighed and stuffed her hands in her pockets. "Man, I could use a cigarette. I wish I smoked..." Then, "They are both probable, but they are both impossible. Unless Mick was not with Jennifer at the crime scene."

I nodded, chewing my lip. "I thought of that. But even if he pulled that off—and the risk of exposure by a handful of other cops, plus the ME and the crime scene team would be huge—even if he pulled that off, he needs at least two other guys with him to pull the trigger. The only person who can have done it is Carlitos." I shook my head. "But I know he didn't."

She looked at her watch and slapped me on the shoulder. "We been hungover and on our feet for almost twenty-four hours, Stone. Let's get a few hours' sleep and come at this again with rested brains. Whadd'ya say?"

"Yeah, you're right."

I turned to go in, but she said, "Hey, Stone...?"

"What?"

"Thanks."

"For what?"

"You almost took a bullet for me tonight."

I was about to dismiss it, but something stopped me. I smiled. "You'd had the same thought, Carmen. I was lucky I was a couple of steps ahead of you."

She smiled. "You're okay, Stone. You're a fucking dinosaur, but you're okay."

"Don't get sentimental on me, Dehan. I'll think you're going soft!"

I had to shout the last couple of words, because she was already walking across the lot toward her car.

Sixteen

I SLEPT FIVE HOURS, then phoned Dehan at lunchtime to tell her to pack a bag and, when she was ready, to go over to my place. We'd be setting out before dawn next morning; it was a twenty-four-hour drive to Shamrock. Then I went over to the precinct and went up to see the captain. I knocked, but I didn't wait for an answer. I stepped in and closed the door. She stared at me. I sat.

"Using my dinosaur methods, last night we got confessions from two of the leading Sureños. We took down two members of a Mexican cartel, and we gathered sufficient evidence to hand over to the Feds so they can mount a major cross-state operation."

"Congratulations, Stone, but spare me the sarcasm, please."

I ignored her. "What we didn't get was a confession regarding Nelson."

She shrugged. "It's a ten-year-old case. If Sam couldn't..."

"I'll spare you the sarcasm, if you'll spare me the bullshit." She closed her mouth, and her eyes shone with anger. "I have statements from half a dozen people to the effect that Mick was a bent cop taking money from local organized crime, and the Mob and the Triads. I have bank records that show that he transferred a total of four million bucks to Belize in the year before he disappeared. I have evidence that he changed his name and used forged documents to go to Mexico. And I have his fingerprints, under a different name, in Shamrock, Texas, on a drunk and disorderly charge ten years ago, two nights after he disappeared. He disappeared after drinking tequila with somebody the night that Nelson was killed. The night he was on duty with you."

Throughout my speech, she had been staring out of the window at the trees across the road. Now she shook her head and looked at me like she wanted to hit me.

"Jesus, Stone, you are a pain in my ass."

"Yeah? A lot of people feel that way about me, Jennifer. But believe me, this is just the beginning. Now, I'm all for keeping the peace and not rocking the boat. That partner you gave me, however, is a bit more aggressive. I have to congratulate you on creating a killer team."

"What do you want, Stone?"

"I want to know why you are covering for Mick. I want to know what went on—or goes on—between you two. I want to know what happened that night. I *want* to know if Mick killed Nelson. And last but not least, I want to go to Shamrock and talk to the county sheriff."

"You are blackmailing me."

I shook my head. "There is nothing unjustified about the threat I'm making, Jennifer. I am trying to do my job, and if you stand in my way, I will take you down, according to the letter of the law. I'm giving you the opportunity to clear yourself and do the right thing."

"You son of a bitch." I went to stand. "Wait!"

I sat. She sighed and looked down at her fingers, like she had memories hanging from them.

"Mick and I had an affair. He was a total son of a bitch. But he had magnetism and that Irish charm. I couldn't resist him. It lasted, on and off, for about a year, the last year he was here. For him it was just a game, but for me it was a lot more than that. I was in love with him.

"A week or so before he disappeared, his partner, Kirk, called in sick. So Mick suggested to the lieutenant that we could partner up. I was new and he was the most experienced detective on the squad. We worked together for about a week. It was probably the happiest week of my life."

She looked embarrassed. "So what happened that night?" I asked.

She gave a small shrug. "Somebody reported a shooting on Longwood Avenue, near the railway tracks, about one or two in the morning. It was a young guy, early twenties."

"Who identified him?"

She frowned a moment. "He had his ID on him. Later his mother identified him."

"How was he killed?"

"Shot in the head. It was an execution. Why?"

"This kid was a student from Brooklyn, why would they execute him?"

She spread her hands. "He'd been at José's tavern, up the road, boasting he was going to kill Nelson. He wanted to know where Nelson was. Some guy in the bar said he would take him. He must have led him down the road and shot him."

I knew the answer, but I asked anyway. "Did you catch the guy who did it?"

"No. You know what it's like. They clam up. Nobody saw anything, nobody heard anything."

"Who was your witness?"

She shrugged. "A young Latino kid. But as soon as we started asking questions, he said he didn't know anything and left."

I sighed. "You didn't hold him and check him for GSR?"

"No."

"The only witness you had to a homicide and you let him walk away."

"Get off my back, Stone!"

I could feel myself getting mad. "I don't know if you are engaged in a big, fucking cover-up, Jennifer, or if you are simply criminally incompetent."

"*How dare you!*"

"I dare. And don't push me, because the only person in this room looking at early retirement is you, Captain." I sank back in my chair and thought while she stared at me, teetering between rage and fear. After a moment, I asked her, "Did you go back to Mick's house with him that night?"

"No. He didn't want me to. He said me he was going to be gone for a bit, and to tell people he'd gone to Miami for his health."

"And you dutifully covered for him."

She nodded. "For ten years."

I watched her a moment, then asked, "How much did you know?"

She pulled a face. "I knew he was bent. I didn't know how bent. I didn't want to know."

"Did you know he was in with the Mob?"

She wouldn't meet my eye. "No. I didn't know any details at all."

I stood. "I'm going down to Shamrock for a couple of days. I want you to call the Wheeler sheriff's department as a courtesy. Tell them we're coming and ask them to cooperate with us. When I get back, you and me are going to talk. I want you out of this job. Ideally, I want you out of the NYPD. But there is no way in hell that you are staying on as captain. Either you go, or I'll kick your ass from here to Belize."

She didn't answer. I left.

I checked a few things I needed to confirm and headed home at about five. I was thinking of a big steak and a bottle of beer and then an early night. I was pretty beat and still had a lingering hangover, and we had a twenty-four-hour drive ahead of us. I was wondering what time Dehan would show up as I pulled into my road, and saw her sitting on the hood of her car, waiting for me. I parked behind her and climbed out. It was good to see her.

"Do you own a frying pan?" she asked.

"I'm not sure."

"I brought some Argentinean beef."

I walked up the steps toward my door. "And you plan to cook it? Isn't that a crime?" I opened the door and stood back to let her in. She slid off the hood of her car and climbed the stairs at a little run. "We can do better. We can scorch it over a barbeque."

"You're a good man, John Stone. You're a good man."

Seventeen

WE DIDN'T TALK MUCH during the drive because while I was driving she was sleeping, and while she was driving I was sleeping, but as we moved steadily south and west, along the I-70 and then from St Louis, the I-44, slowly, everything began to fit into place. I tried it from every angle, but I couldn't find a flaw. I needed evidence—I needed proof. There were things I needed to see with my own eyes. But it was as clear to me in my mind, as though I had been there and seen it happen. I played it over, again and again as we drove through the day and then through the night; and as we passed Oklahoma the vast, flat horizon began to pale behind us, in the east.

At Weatherford, in Custer County, I pulled into a service station and woke Dehan. It was seven in the morning, and the sky was lighting up, though the sun hadn't yet risen. We ordered eggs and bacon and pancakes, and sat eating and drinking coffee in sleepy silence till ten to eight. Then I called the sheriff to tell him we were a couple of hours from Shamrock.

He had the slow drawl you'd expect from a Texan, and he told me he'd be mighty obliged if I'd go to Wheeler, which was where he was based, and he'd be happy to answer any questions we had. I told him that would be fine, and a couple of hours later, at nine a.m., we rolled into his town. It was already getting hot.

It was a town that didn't really have streets. It was more like there were houses and barns and buildings, and areas of grass and woodland, scattered sparsely in a grid pattern over an area of countryside. The sheriff's office was a big old redbrick building, vaguely reminiscent of the Wild West, more or less at the center of the grid. It stood alone, twenty yards from the general store on one side, and a hundred yards from the nearest house on the other. Space was something they were not short of in Wheeler, Texas.

We parked out front next to the sheriff's pickup and went inside. It was a big room with a high ceiling and a wooden floor. There were a couple of desks, one of them by a tall window at the back. That was the only one that was occupied. The sheriff stood as we came in and walked toward us with slow, deliberate steps. Space and time were both abundant here.

He held out his hand and smiled.

"Detectives Stone and Dehan? Sheriff Ted Weiss, at your service, ma'am." This last was directed at Dehan. "Come on in and make yourselves at home. I have some coffee brewing, if you'd like some."

We told him we were fine, and he drew up a couple of chairs to his desk. There was a file open where he'd been sitting. It wasn't thick, just a couple of pages. We all sat, and he leaned back and regarded me with just a hint or that irony that Texans reserve especially for New Yorkers.

"You're looking for someone and you think we found him?"

"Them, perhaps. Like I said on the phone, we got a hit on IAFIS. Ten years ago, you arrested a man in Shamrock..."

"Michael O'Hannafin. More Irish than the Irish. I was just refreshing my memory. I've been sheriff here for fifteen years. I remember the man. He was a loudmouth. He got drunk and wanted to show everybody how tough he was. He said he was on his way to Mexico, but he talked like a New Yorker. I didn't ask him a lot of questions. To be honest I wasn't interested. I figured if he was going on his way, that was good enough for me."

I nodded. "Sure. Was he traveling alone?"

"Nope. He had a young Mexican girl with him. Sweet kid. She was polite and pretty, couldn't have been more than twenty. I couldn't figure out what a girl like that was doing with an old thug like him." He shrugged. "Takes all sorts, I guess."

I scratched my chin. "She made no effort to talk to you alone, no plea for help...?" I shook my head, shrugged. "Nothing of that sort?"

He frowned. "Well, no... You telling me she was abducted?"

"I don't know. We aren't sure yet. But it's possible."

"Shoot."

"How long were they in town, Sheriff?"

"They arrived that morning. They booked in to the Sleep Inn on 66, and then they went to Big Vern's for a steak dinner. Vern does his own brand beer. It's good beer and it looks like your friend Michael took a liking to it."

"He got drunk?"

He studied my face for a moment, with his fingers laced across his belly. "Shamrock is a quiet town, Detective. By eleven just about everything is closed and folks go home. We like it that way. This Michael didn't. He'd had a few beers too many, and he was making a noise about how this wasn't no Irish town. The Irish knew how to drink, that kind of stuff. The staff asked him to keep it down, and he became abusive." He looked down at his fingers and raised an eyebrow at them. "Vern's is a family restaurant. I can recommend the steak. You won't find any better anywhere. It's a real friendly, family place." He looked up and held my eye. "I know it's a different world out east. But here we don't like swearing, especially in front of ladies. We got different values."

Dehan smiled and said, "Somebody told him to watch his mouth?"

He nodded. "Couple of boys took him outside, and things could have got ugly. Luckily I was in the area, and when Vern called, I swung by and brought him up here to sleep it off."

"What about Maria?"

"The girl? She went back to their room. She was awful upset, kept apologizing and crying her eyes out. Broke my heart to see it."

Dehan asked, "And next day?"

"He was pleasant enough. Apologized. Didn't seem all that sincere, but at least it was gracious. We took his prints, but when he said he was fixin' to leave town and move down to Mexico with his wife, I didn't see the point in taking things any further." He frowned again and looked at me and Dehan curiously. "What I don't understand, Detectives, is, if she was abducted, when he was cooling off in the cell overnight, why didn't she ask us for help? Or simply take off? Why did she wait for him?"

"That," I said, "is a very good question.

We stood and he stood with us. He said, "You going to be staying long?"

I smiled. "Just a couple of days. I promise to be in bed by eleven." I hesitated. "Have you any record of what he was driving?"

He picked up a file from his desk. "Your captain phoned as a courtesy. Nice lady. We had a laugh. She asked me to give you any help I could. Well, we'd do that anyway. I copied the file for you. Anything we know is in there." He handed it to me. "Red 1969 Ford Mustang Mach 1 V8, bigger'n Texas."

Dehan sighed. "Of course he was."

The sheriff gave his head a little tweak. "Nice car, nice girl, shame about the dork."

He stepped outside with us into the bright morning sunshine. "You got a few motels along the famous route 66—it passes through Shamrock. You got a couple of hotels too. If I can be of any help, just let me know." He smiled at Dehan. "People round here are pretty friendly, as long as you don't tell them they ain't Irish enough."

We climbed in the Jag and headed south on 83 through flat semi-desert. The land was dry, but there was an abundance of trees, and I guessed that during the rainy season it was probably green and fertile. Dehan was quiet for a while, but after ten minutes she asked, "What are you thinking? You have the answer, don't you?"

"I don't know yet."

"You're lying."

"I know." She looked at me. "Just give me a day. Humor me. I'm not sure."

"So what are we doing? We know he was here. We know Maria was with him. We know she was with him voluntarily..."

"Maybe."

"What do you mean, maybe? She could have left and she didn't."

I sucked my teeth. "Maybe."

She stared ahead through the windshield at the long straight road and said in an exasperated voice, "Will you at least tell me what we're doing here?"

I nodded. "Yeah. We're looking for a Red 1969 Ford Mustang Mach 1, V8."

She didn't react for a bit. Then she turned and stared at me, and I could see the flat Texas morning landscape starkly reflected in her aviators.

Eighteen

WE FORWENT THE IRISH Inn and the Blarney Inn and plumbed for the "retro-themed, modestly priced" Route 66. Perhaps it was the rebel in me. We booked two rooms next to each other, and after we'd showered and changed our clothes, I called Dehan in and made a plan. She sat cross-legged on my bed.

"I want to know what kept Maria with Mick. I want to know why she didn't run or appeal to the sheriff for help. So what I want you to do is go to the places she might have gone to. Start at the hotel. See if anybody remembers her. As far as it's possible, we need a record of her movements that day, up until Mick came back from the sheriff's and they left."

She winced. "That was ten years ago. You think people will remember?"

"I'm guessing not a lot happens in a town like this, Dehan. Anything a little out of the ordinary probably gets laid down in the town mythology." I winked and said, "Ah sure, Paddy O'Flaherty's probably written a ballad about it, sure he has!"

She had a way of making no expression really expressive, and she did that now.

"You realize that is really insulting and offensive to Irish people, right?"

I shrugged. "I'm a stereotypic dinosaur. We live up to our stereotypes. Now quit stalling and start walking."

She didn't move. She was a rebel, like me.

"What are you going to do?"

"Drive into the desert and commune with Brother Eagle."

She sighed and left. She didn't know my cousin's great-grandfather once removed was one tenth Cherokee.

I looked briefly at a map. Route 83 took you pretty much in a straight line all the way to Mexico. So I got in my car and started driving south at a leisurely pace. It wasn't really what you could call desert. It was hot and dry because of the time of year, but there were plenty of trees and waterways.

About four miles out of town, I came to a track on my right. It seemed to lead toward some dense woodland, so I turned into it. It wasn't too rough, but I could tell the Jag wasn't enjoying it all that much. I bumped along for a bit until I saw a big Dodge RAM rolling toward me. I stopped and got out to wait for it to arrive. It pulled up twenty feet in front of me, and a big man in his fifties got out and smiled at me.

"That's a nice car you got there," he said. "I'd like to ask you what it's doing on my land."

He wasn't unfriendly. He was just to the point. I made a note in my mind not to question his Irishness. I smiled back and held out my hand. He shook it and I told him my name.

"I'm with the NYPD."

He raised an eyebrow. "You're an awful long way from home, Mr. Stone."

I noticed he didn't call me detective. I wasn't a detective in his state.

"I'm here at the invitation of your sheriff. We're looking for a couple of people who went missing ten years back." I made a face like what I was saying wasn't exactly accurate and added, "In fact, I'm looking for their car, which may have been dumped around these parts ten years ago. A '69 Mustang Mach 1."

He laughed. "I can tell you here and now I didn't find it, or my wife would be driving it right now." He shook his head and stood staring at the land around him, at the huge horizon. "No," he said. "These lands south of Shamrock are well cared for, Mr. Stone. Car like that would've been found, and everybody would've heard about it. You're looking in the wrong place."

I nodded and thanked him and went to turn back to my car. He gave a small grunt of a laugh and pointed at the Jag. "You're looking in the wrong place, with the wrong vehicle. You want something that'll go off road."

I smiled. "I'm a New Yorker. I don't ride."

"Not a horse. Get a truck. You can rent one over in Texola at Ted's place, fourteen mile east back the way you came on I-40."

I thought about it for a moment, and all of a sudden, ideas started to slot into place. "That makes sense." Then, on an impulse: "Say, I'm guessing you know these parts pretty well. If you wanted to hide a car so nobody would find it, where would you put it?"

He crossed his arms and raised an eyebrow. "Besides a lockup? I wouldn't bring it down here, down south. Like I said, these lands are worked and well tended." He pulled a face. "I figure I'd take out west, toward Amarillo. Armstrong County, maybe Donley, south and west of Clarendon, to the Palo Duro Canyon. That's the sort of territory I'd be looking for. 'Bout sixty mile west of here."

I thanked him and left. In my mirror I could see him watching me with his hands on his hips. I knew he was amused.

I followed his advice and drove to Texola. Texola was like Wheeler, only more so. There was a grid pattern of roads with nothing between them except the odd house or a shed, or sometimes a farm. I found Ted's place easy enough. It was a big wooden barn that had things painted on it in red and white paint, like "wheel change" and "oil."

I pulled off the road and killed the engine. An old guy in overalls came out of the shed, wiping his hands on a cloth that seemed to be making his hands dirtier than they were. He was staring at my car.

"Hi, are you Ted?"

He studied my face as though the question amused him and said, "Nice car."

"Thanks. I need to hire a truck for a few days, a Jeep or a pickup."

"Foreign. They din't make that in Dee-troit!" He laughed like he'd cracked a real funny joke. I chuckled and said a little more forcefully, "Can I rent a truck from you?"

"Sure y'can." He turned and started to walk away. "Long as you don't lose the darn thing. Don't know how you can lose a darn truck. Big as Texas."

I followed him into the cool shade of the barn structure. There was a Ford pickup and next to it a Dodge RAM.

"I got them insured, but that don't mean you can just take off with 'em. Still puts m'darn premium up, don'it?"

"I'm not planning to make off with your truck, Ted. I just want to hire it for a day or two."

He nodded past me at my car. "Whatcha fixin' to do with your car?"

I hadn't thought it through. I'd had some vague notion of coming out again with Dehan. He said, "I can take it for ya. I done that before, but then you gotta bring me back, aintcha?"

"Clean her up. Check the oil. I'll come back for it this evening."

He shrugged. "Suit yerself. I won't do nothin' fancy. It's a foreign car, ain'it?"

There was no paperwork involved, as long as I paid cash and promised to bring the truck back. I did both and five minutes later I was driving west along the I-40 toward Amarillo. I drove for about an hour, and then in Donley County, I turned left onto the State Highway 70. As the farmer at Shamrock had suggested, this was a lot more promising. The short distance had made a difference. The landscape was parched. The earth was brown turning to a dirty, desiccated gray. And as I headed south on route 70, the terrain to my right—to the west—began to fall away into valleys and deep hollows.

It was promising, but it was also vast. It was going to take time—time I didn't have a lot of. I drove for about fifteen minutes without seeing any paths to the right or left that tempted me to explore. Eventually I came to Hardwick and the Greenbelt reservoir. There was a kind of trailer park down there with dirt tracks running off in all directions around the lake. I spent the rest of the afternoon exploring every one of them. I discovered that they all led to the same place. Nowhere.

By six o'clock I was beat, and I headed back to the Route 66 Inn. I picked up Dehan and took her to collect my Jaguar. When we got back and I had showered ten hours of sweat and dust off my body, she strolled into my room without knocking and sat on my bed. Fortunately I had most of my clothes on.

"Get dressed, Sensei. I'm taking you out to dinner. This town has a place called Big Vern's Steak House, with its own brand beer. You realize we may have died and gone to Texas?"

She had a point.

Nineteen

IT WAS PROBABLY THE best steak I had ever eaten in my life, and it kept Dehan intensely quiet for a full fifteen minutes. When she'd finished, she sat back, licked her lips, and said, "That right there was not a steak. That was an experience. Moments like that make life worthwhile." I smiled. She didn't. "I'm serious."

She drained her beer and waved the empty glass at the waitress. While she waited for a refill, she said, "Now, are you going to tell me why we are looking for Mick's car here?"

I sucked my teeth and sighed. "What did you find out about Maria's movements that day?"

"That would be a no, then."

"My answer depends somewhat on yours."

The waitress appeared with glowing teeth and hair and placed a beer in front of Dehan, who studied it for a while.

"Not a whole lot. No ballads were written about her. Nobody seems to remember much about her at all. Except the manageress at the hotel remembered her because of the whole fight thing. She said Maria did something next day that surprised her."

"She left town midmorning while Mick was still in the county lockup? Asked where she could hire a car?"

Dehan made a funny little jerk with her head and closed her eyes, like she had three or four different questions and didn't know which one to ask first. There was a smile too, but not a very amused one. In the end, she said, "What... like... how...?"

"Lucky guess. What did the woman tell her—Texola?"

She shrugged. "I could just go back to New York and take up sewing."

"Don't be silly. Who would I show off to, then?"

She studied my face while I studied the tablecloth.

"Okay, Stone, you're a clever man, there is no denying that. But suddenly I can sense where you're going with this, and I just don't buy it."

"Good. Tell me where I'm going, and where I'm going wrong."

She slung an arm over the back of her chair and pointed at me.

"You're developing this idea of Maria as a kind of Lucrezia Borgia-cum-Machiavelli who manipulates Mick into arranging the killing of Nelson, and then induces him to get drunk and arrested here, and while he's in the slammer she hires a car, has it waiting somewhere, kills him, leaves him in the car, and makes off with the cash."

I gave my head a little sideways nod and thought about it. "What's wrong with it?"

"To start with, her. In all the descriptions we've had of her, she's never been described as manipulative, ruthless, or capable of homicide. She is, or was, sweet and submissive. She was a good girl at home with her mom, she cared for her brother. She was going straight into marriage at age twenty..."

"To somebody of another faith."

"Minor point. When Nelson said no, she obeyed and married him. When Nelson said go with Mick, she went with Mick. When Mick said come escape with me, she went. The picture I get of this girl is a typical, submissive, obedient Catholic girl."

"Okay, good point. What else?"

"To organize a successful murder is a difficult and complicated thing. To organize a murder where the body, and a red 1969 Mustang, disappear for ten years is a *really* complicated thing. You need to know the territory. You need to know the good places to hide the body. You need to know the customs of the people around you—who is likely to find it? How can I avoid them? She's a kid from the Bronx! What does she know about Texas?"

"Also very good points. Anything else?"

"Yeah, killing a two-hundred-and-forty-pound Irish cop is not easy. How did she do it? How did she get him in the car? How did she dispose of him?" She shook her head a lot. "I can't see any way that it works, Stone."

I nodded. "They are all excellent points."

"You want to hear my theory?"

"Always."

"I have to tell you it hasn't changed a whole lot, except now it comes in two parts. First, I think we have to accept that Mick killed Nelson."

I frowned. "We know he wasn't there."

"I mean he was responsible. His idea was to cause confusion and make some extra dough by selling the information about the poker game to the Mob and the Triads. He takes the precaution a week before the hit of sending Kirk off sick. Really what Kirk is doing is preparing the hit with a couple of free-lance pros. That explains why the dope wasn't taken. They're professionals. They take the dope, and that's a trail that can lead the cops to their door. They don't need it, they don't take it."

I nodded. "That's good."

"Kirk takes the money and Maria to Mick's house, then beats it to Yonkers, where he leads the quiet life and nobody ever hears from him again. Mick and Maria have a shot of tequila and head for Mexico. As you correctly anticipated, he gets into trouble along the way. Why doesn't she leave him when he's in the slammer? Because she is terrified of him. She knows he'll track her down and beat seven bails of shit out of her. She waits patiently for him to come out, and they drive on to Mexico. Once over the border, he does the same thing again, because that is his nature. They stop at some village where the local boss is the law. Mick starts mouthing off, flashing his car and his money. But this time, instead of getting thrown in the can by the local sheriff, they both get knifed and some Mexican *patron* gets his money and his car. Pretty Latina girls? They got plenty of them in Mexico."

"Superb. Nine out of ten."

"Nine out of ten...?"

"Why did she ask about renting a car?"

She hunched her shoulders and spread her hands like I was being absurd.

"That's not so hard to explain, Stone! She thought about running back to New York, or somewhere else. Who wouldn't? But she panicked at the last moment and couldn't see it through."

I made a face. "You certainly seem to have covered all the angles. So how do we set about proving it?"

She gave a small humorless laugh, "Ay, there's the rub..." She watched me watching her a moment, then said, "That's a quote."

"And a very appropriate one, because he is wondering what comes after death. We can only speculate what came after their deaths. Because we don't know. And that's the recurring theme, isn't it? A perfect theory, with no evidence. Two murders in which the killings leave us with plenty of theory, but no trail to follow."

"And you think that's deliberate."

"Yup."

"I just don't see Maria planning something as cunning and twisted as that... It's not *her*."

I sighed. "I know. You may be right. Give me another day. Let's see what we find in Armstrong County tomorrow."

Her eyes lit up in mock excitement.

"Oh, can I come along tomorrow? Sure you don't want me to question the shopkeepers so then you can tell me what I found out?"

I shook my head. "Been there. Done that."

"Cute."

We stepped out of the restaurant, and Dehan stopped to look up at the stars. There was no moon, and it was like looking at a billion tiny shards of ice scattered over a deep, translucent ocean.

"We don't see that back home, do we, Stone?"

"Nope."

It was less than a half mile walk back to the inn, and it was a perfect temperature, with a cool breeze coming in off the plains. She walked with her hands in her pockets, watching her boots as they took each step.

"I think I know why you won't tell me your theory."

"Assuming I have a theory."

"You have. I think you are vain. Like the song, you know? I bet you think this song is aboutcha, dontcha?" She laughed out loud. "You can't bear the thought that you might tell me your theory..."

"Assuming I have a theory."

"...and it might be wrong. Go on. Admit it."

"I have a certain intellectual vanity..."

She mimicked my voice. "I have a certain intellectual vanity..." She burst out laughing again. "You're cool, Stone. I'll let you off. But when you start all that 'Ha! It is as I suspected!' bullshit, *you'll* know that *I* know that you *didn't* know..."

We had reached her door, and her eyes were bright in the starlight. I smiled. "Good try. But I repeat: I have no theory. I know. I know *almost* everything. And with a little luck, I will confirm it tomorrow. And then, Miss Cocky Pants, you'll be laughing on the other side of your face."

I opened my door and stepped in.

"Good night, Dehan."

As I closed the door, I heard her parting words.

"I still say you're vain."

Twenty

I LAY FOR A LONG WHILE that night, staring at the ceiling and running over her theory. It was good. It made a lot of sense. It was elegant and simple. I weighed it against my own conclusions. Was she right? Was it vanity? Or something else?

We started out early, as the sun was rising in the east and before the heat started sapping the life out of everything it touched. We drove west toward Amarillo for about an hour and a half, staring at the endless expanses of dry flatness. Dehan was looking like she was trying hard to hold on to her patience. I didn't let that distract me. I was trying to imagine what had been going through Mick and Maria's minds as they drove along this road ten years ago.

Finally she couldn't keep her mouth shut any longer, and she said, "This is route 66..."

I smiled. "That's where we get our kicks, Dehan."

"It's I-40, and it leads to Los Angeles."

"You want to go to California, hang out with the beautiful people?" She didn't answer. She just looked at me through her shades and waited. "You think we should go south, toward Mexico?"

She cocked her head on one side and did something that was never intended to be a smile.

We had reached the turnoff for the 207 down to Claude. I pulled off right, then followed the loop over the bridge, and then we were driving dead south. The landscape was still about as flat and featureless as you could get without sandpapering it.

"Stone..." She was sounding now like it wasn't really amusing anymore. She gestured at the thousands of square miles of emptiness. "The only thing you could hide out here is corn, or dirt—flat dirt! Come on! Give it up! How can you hide a red Mustang in this, for crying out loud?"

I scratched my chin. She said, "Listen to me. The car is in Mexico!"

We drove in to Claude and out the other end again, and everything was still flat when we got there. After another five or six miles, little had changed, except that we had gone over a small rise, once. Then I said, "When you look around you, you'd think that this endless, featureless landscape would go on forever. But here is the advantage of being a little studious and using your imagination, not to mention maps..."

She raised an eyebrow at me. I pointed up ahead. "See where the road bears right up ahead?" She glanced, curious in spite of herself. "See what happens when we get there."

We got there and she shrugged. "So the road bent. I agree, out here that is like a major event. But..."

"Climb off..."

"What?"

"Your high horse. Climb off it. Look again." I slowed right down and pointed left. "See the land over there? Flat, featureless, and fertile. Now look over on your right. The earth is turning gray. It's scrubland, small gnarled bushes. Now, as we proceed further round the bend, what do you notice...?"

She was frowning. "Okay... The landscape is changing. We have a deep valley opening up here on the right. But I don't see..."

"Oh, little grasshopper!" I said, "You see, but you do not *imagine*!"

"Give me strength..."

I pointed up ahead again. "Now, you see up there? The road turns left. Let's see what happens there..."

She stared at me a while. The expression in her eyes was hidden by her large, reflective aviators. She said, "Is it like this in your head all the time?"

"You should join me. It's fun." We turned the bend, and I exclaimed, "Oh, by golly, by gum! What have we here?" I did a fair imitation of a Texan and said, "Ah do believe, Detective Dee-han, that we are in a canyon!"

Before us, the interminable flatness had been suddenly replaced by a vast sweep of deep valleys and rolling hills. The earth began to turn now from gray to red, as though it had been rusted through the millennia. An abundance of bushes and small trees dotted the landscape among rough, hardy shrubs. The road continued to bend and curve as it descended.

"We are now entering, Detective Carmen Dehan, the Palo Duro Canyon, said to be the second largest in the USA. At the bottom, in about five minutes, we shall find the Prairie Dog Town Fork of the Red River, and then we shall begin to climb up, onto the far side of the canyon."

"Shall we?"

"Indeed."

The river was less impressive than its name. It was more like a very large trickle of mud. We crossed it via a concrete bridge and slowly began to climb up the far side. Dehan had gone quiet, and I was watching the roadside, waiting to see something that would tell me I had found the place. I saw it after about five minutes. It was an esplanade, just before a small bridge that crossed a broad track. The track wound its way down into the canyon and was lost among juniper bushes and mesquite. I slowed right down, spun the wheel, and eased off the road and down onto the track.

It must have been about ten a.m. by then, and it was getting hot. As we bumped down along, clouds of fine red-and-gray dust rose up around us. But there was no breeze to carry them away, so they just lingered and followed us, like sleepy, lonely ghosts that had been abandoned in the desert too long.

We bounced and rattled down the track for about fifteen minutes, with the sides of the canyon growing steeper and narrower around us the deeper we sank. As we proceeded I began to realize that it wasn't really a track at all, but a dry river bed. And after a quarter of an hour, we came to a place where a second, smaller river joined this bigger one. I figured they only flowed in the rainy season. I stopped and sat staring. The banks and the slopes were overgrown, but the bed itself was clear. There were rocks but no growth.

"When is the rainy season in the Panhandle, Dehan?"

She shook her head. "I have no idea."

"May and June. The water must come down there at quite a rate, washing everything away. That's why the watercourse is clear of vegetation, while the sides are overgrown. December, there is very little rain here."

"Really..."

"Yup."

I killed the engine and climbed out. I started scrambling up the dry tributary and heard the truck door slam behind me. We scrambled and climbed for about five minutes toward a dense clump of juniper bushes that had grown up around a sharp bend in the stream. I could imagine that during the rainy season a lot of water accumulated there, making that spot especially fertile. I thought about explaining that to Dehan but decided to leave it till later, over a beer.

I stopped about twenty yards from the thicket. You could see clearly where, over the years, the water had carved out a new course for itself to get around the obstruction. Dehan came and stood next to me, panting slightly and perspiring, with her hands on her hips. She was quiet for a long time. Finally she said, "Son of a bitch."

I grinned at her and said, "Ha! It is as I thought!"

She ignored me and we clambered the remaining few yards. A decade of heat and rain had taken its toll on the car. The red paint was faded, and there was a lot of corrosion. The windows were down, and I peered in. Dehan leaned in the other side. It was hard to be sure at a glance. There was no telling how many times the car had been flooded with fast-moving water over the years. Dehan, not for the first time, spoke my thoughts aloud.

"You've got air and you've got water, so you've got bacteria, and so, fast decomposition. Plus, you have all kinds of wild animals. There are going to be bits of them all over this canyon. But I'd lay money on a man and a woman."

I nodded, staring at the passenger seat. There was a small collection of bones on the floor and what looked like a thigh bone on the seat. I said, "We should leave it untouched and get the forensic anthropologist to have a look at it. But I just want to have a glance..." I pulled open the door and peered in the back. There were bones back there too, mainly small to medium. I made a mental note, then leaned down and looked under the passenger seat. It was there. I got my handkerchief, reached in, and carefully pulled it out. A skull. The lower jaw was barely hanging on, but it was there. Dehan watched me as I set it on the roof of the car and photographed the teeth from several angles. Then I put it back where I had found it.

The other skull was smaller, and it was wedged under the driver's seat. I did the same, then put it back where I'd found it. "The positions of the skulls don't tell us much, because water and animals may have moved them around several times, but it's interesting his skull was under the passenger seat."

I found the release button and popped the trunk. I closed the driver's door and walked to the back.

There was nothing much to see except a spare wheel, a tool case, and an old sports bag. Dehan was by my side staring in. I glanced at her. "You done?"

She nodded and I closed it. I stayed a while, leaning against the car and gazing down along the desiccated channel among the dusty junipers. I said, "We haven't got long. We have to report this, and as soon as we do, it goes over to the bureau. That gives us twenty-four, forty-eight hours at the outside."

"What the hell were they doing? It's a miracle they got the car here at all! Why would you do that?" She scowled at me, like Mick and Maria and I had all got it wrong. "He's going to Mexico—we at least agree he was headed for Mexico?"

I nodded. "Yes, he was headed for Mexico."

"So *why*, instead of driving directly south on 83, out of Shamrock, straight to the Mexican border, does he go maybe a hundred miles out of his way to the Palo Duro Canyon and take his beloved, priceless, 1969 Mustang down a dry riverbed?"

I shook my head and held up my hand. "Stop."

She didn't. She went on, "And more than that, Stone, how in the name of *holy fuck* did you know he did that?"

"Stop, Dehan. Stop." We stared at each other a moment. "Detective Carmen Dehan would not do that. Detective Carmen Dehan is a very smart cookie and thinks in a logical, systematic way. She suits her thoughts and her actions to her intentions. But we are not after Detective Dehan. So stop thinking like Detective Dehan, and start thinking like the person you are hunting."

"More dinosaur shit."

"What does Mick want?"

"Okay, okay..." She walked away from me and stood with her hands on her hips, looking out at the glare of the canyon. She made a nice silhouette. She spoke without looking at me. "He wants what he's always wanted, to rule the roost, to show off, to intimidate. He wants to display his power, his wealth, his cute chick, his car." She turned to face me. "But I still don't see..."

I interrupted her. "But you *do* see that, given that his prime motivation was *not* to cross the Mexican border, it would not be so difficult to draw him a hundred miles off his route."

"Yeah... I see that. But who...?"

"That, *that* is the question. Who? Not why, but who."

In the truck, as we bumped and scrambled our way back toward the road, she said, "Right from the start, there has been the presence in this case of an unknown person."

I nodded. "Yup."

"And you saw it from the beginning, didn't you?"

"Yup."

"When you did your little acting out of the murder on day one—" She imitated my voice. "—'Good evening, gentlemen, nothing to be alarmed about...' you were thinking to yourself, 'There is somebody here we can't see...'"

I laughed. "I guess so."

"That person lured them here and killed them." She shook her head and rubbed her face. "Stone, I have to admit, I am even more confused now than I was before we found the car and the bodies. We are looking at *exactly* the same question we were looking at from the word go. Who is this unknown person? The only difference is now we're asking it about seven bodies instead of five."

I sighed. "Looks that way."

She went silent then, and I drove back the way we'd come, but instead of going directly to Shamrock I took the 83 to Wheeler and dropped in on the sheriff. He smiled at us as we stepped into his big, shady office and said, "You still here? I hope you ain't causin' trouble."

"Not at all. I compliment everybody I meet on how Irish they are. Actually, we will be leaving very soon. I just wanted your guidance on a matter of jurisdiction."

He frowned at me and crossed his arms. "Tell me."

"We were just exploring the Palo Duro Canyon. We thought it would be a shame to come this far..."

"Yeah, yeah, I get you. What did you find out there?"

"We happened to spot a red 1969 Mustang stuck in a dry riverbed, about three miles past the bridge on the 207."

We stared at each other for a long time. Finally, he said, "Son of a gun... Well, that's Armstrong County..."

"Exactly. Now here is what I am thinking, Sheriff. There are what appear to be human remains in the car."

He said, "Mick Harragan, aka Michael O'Hannafin, and Maria Garcia."

"Looks that way. It is also looking very much as though he was responsible for at least five murders and one abduction on *my* turf, plus a lot of corruption and racketeering."

He was nodding before I finished. "Sooner or later you have to hand this over to the Feds and they're gonna take over your case. Well..." He gave me a knowing look. "I know you are mighty anxious to do that as soon as possible, but we have to observe all the correct formalities." He had a twinkle in his eye that told me we were on the same page. "I am no expert in jurisdiction, Stone, but I think you should leave it to me to contact Sheriff Oats out in Armstrong, get his opinion on the matter, and then I suppose he'll need a statement from you, which he will submit through the appropriate channels."

I smiled. "That sounds about right."

We shook hands and headed back toward the Route 66 Inn in Shamrock. As we turned into the parking lot, Dehan said, "Well, whaddaya know, Stone? We got a visit from the Mob. Were you expecting this?"

I shook my head. "No."

There was a dark blue Audi 8 parked by the door, and as we pulled up, Vito, dressed in his best Armani, got out and opened the back door for Pro. He waved at us and said, "Where you been? I been waiting for you!"

Twenty-One

WE SAT IN MY ROOM. Vito stayed outside in the car. Dehan sat on the bed, Pro had the chair, and I sat with my ass on the chest of drawers.

I said, "What are you doing here, Pro?"

"What can I tell you? I live down the road. I heard there's a guy who does a good steak here. His name is Big Vern, or was it Big Paddy? I heard he does his own beer too. But this place—Shamrock! I ask you? It's full of Micks everywhere. Do you think this Big Vern's beer is green? I never had green beer. Not even on St Paddy's Day. Real Irish. Everything is fuckin' Irish. Place must be crawlin' with Micks. You find any Micks since you been here, Stone?"

Dehan said, "Down the road. Five hundred miles down the road, as the crow flies. How the fuck did you know we were here?"

He looked sad and made an expressive gesture with his hands. "Such a shame. Such a pretty face, such an ugly mouth. Who taught you to talk like that?"

"People like you. Answer the question. How did you know we were here?"

"Guys like me, you know, we hear things. You don't always remember who told you what. Sometimes it's one person, sometimes it's another. Somebody said to me, 'Hey! You know what? Stone is over in Shamrock!' I said to myself, 'What is a guy of Stone's qualities and abilities doing in a two-bit town like Shamrock?' So I thought I'd come over and see how you was getting on." He gave me the dead eye for five seconds and asked, "Did you find the motherfucker or not?"

I shook my head, but before I could say anything he was talking again.

"I know you found something, because you been out all fuckin' day. I know you weren't admiring the fuckin' view, 'cause there ain't one. So what are you doing here, Stone? We had a deal, remember?"

It was Dehan who answered, which seemed to irritate Pro. "You don't listen, do you, Morry? You got this crazy thing going on in your head, babbling away, and that's all you hear. So when a cop tells you, 'we ain't going to hand over a suspect to you or provide you with information about him,' that doesn't fit with your head babble, so you don't hear it."

I smiled. She'd nailed it. Pro looked at her a moment, turned to me, and said, "So you have found something?"

"What do you expect us to find, Pro?"

He shrugged. "I don't know. *Did* you find anything?"

"Here's what I don't understand, Pro. I'll tell you what. We'll do a trade. You explain this to me, to my satisfaction, and I will share what I have found with you."

I saw Dehan glance at me and frown, but I ignored her. Pro shrugged and said, "Shoot."

"When we came to visit you in Port Lavaca, you said to me that all I had to do was, and I quote, 'report to the relevant authorities' and you would do the rest. From which I understood that you and Vincenzo would be duly informed of what I discovered about Mick." He grunted. I went on. "But I step outside of New York and in twenty-four hours you're here like a fly on shit. You're not sitting by the pool waiting for a call from Mick's replacement. You're here, asking me why *I* am here. Explain that to me, and I will tell you what I have learned."

He was silent for a long while. He looked sour and the dark rings under his eyes seemed to grow darker. He glanced at me a couple of times, like he was going to say something, but then looked away again. Dehan was watching him like a cat watching a mouse trying to make up its mind whether to go for the cheese. Suddenly he erupted.

"You know what? You're a suspicious son of a bitch. It's just, it just never crossed my mind he might have come out here, is all! But I saw the name, *Shamrock*—Mick was all about being fuckin' Irish—so I thought maybe you had something. Maybe Mick had moved out here, and I guess I wanted to see the motherfucker before you carted him off to wherever. That's all."

"That's all."

"Yeah! That's all." He looked wounded. "You know? I'm on the right side of the law now. I cooperate with you guys. It would be nice if you would cooperate with me sometimes, instead of always being so fuckin' suspicious."

Dehan snorted. "Vincenzo on the right side of the law too?"

"Listen, young lady." He wagged a finger at her. "You got a big mouth, you know that? You got a fuckin' habit of talking when you ain't being spoken to."

Her eyes were hooded, and for a moment she looked dangerous. She spoke quietly. "You wave that finger at me again, Pro, I'm going to tear it off and shove it up your ass."

"Keep talking, sister, and I'll tell you what I'm gonna shove up your pretty little..."

"Watch your mouth!" I snarled.

His eyes swiveled to me, then back to Dehan and back to me again. He leered. "Oh, that the way it is? I didn't mean no disrespect, Stone."

"Is that your story? That you just wanted to see if Mick was here?"

He shrugged and spread his hands. "What else?"

I nodded. "Okay."

"So share. It's your turn."

"Sure." I smiled. "The beer isn't green. I can recommend it. Close the door on your way out."

"You don't want to do this, Stone."

"You got something to tell me, Pro, tell me. Otherwise get the fuck out of my room."

He waited a moment, then stood. He was real tall and lanky and stooping, with huge hands. With the light from the window behind him, he looked for a moment like a monster from a B movie. He turned and moved to the door. When he was there, he stopped and looked back at me. "You are going to regret this, Stone."

I pointed at him. "I'm being patient, Pro. Right now I am respecting the status quo. But cross the line and I am coming after you and whoever is supplying you with information. Get back in your box, or the whole house of cards comes down."

He stepped out and closed the door. After a moment we heard the sound of his Audi pulling out of the lot and fading into the distance. Dehan stared at the bedcover a moment.

Then she said, "Get back in your box or the whole house of cards comes down?"

I smiled. "Nobody's perfect."

"Isn't that what they call a mixed metaphor?"

"Yes. And a bad one."

"Bad? Bad would be, I smell a rat, but I will nip it in the bud. Or, it's time to bite the bullet and throw in the towel. But, get back in your box or the whole house of cards comes down? Man..."

"You done?"

"Maybe."

"What did he want?"

"What did he want...?" She got off the bed, jumped up and down a couple of times, and started pacing. "He wanted information."

"Good. What information in particular?"

"He wanted to know if we had found Mick."

"But that's not right, is it?"

"No, because he already had channels in place to give him that information if and when we found him. Which was the point you made to him. So he wanted to know... *if we had found something besides Mick!*"

I spread my hands, "Which means?"

"That he knew there was something besides Mick to find. And there was *only one way he could have known that.*" She stared hard at me. I stared back, feeling vaguely unsettled. She was very intense. She went on, slower, "But if he killed Mick and Maria, why the hell would he send us searching for them?" She held up her hand. "Wait! I got this. Pro doesn't do his own dirty work. He arranges for somebody to meet Mick here. Has him whacked, and then the hit man either gets killed on the job or makes off with the stash."

She shook her head. "No, that is too convoluted. It's simpler than that. It was misdirection. He heard we had revived the case. He knew a thorough investigation would eventually lead back to him, and wanted to cover himself by appearing to want Mick found..."

She stared at me again and sighed. I smiled. "Go and have a shower. You'll feel better. We'll eat and talk over dinner."

Twenty-Two

SHE CALLED FOR ME A couple of hours later. She had a hint of lipstick and blue eye shadow. I smiled at her as I stepped out of the room. She was looking this way and that a lot. "You're wearing makeup."

She looked surprised, as though she hadn't known she was wearing it. Then she shrugged. "Yeah, you know, I sometimes, just a bit..."

"Looks nice."

"Yeah. Thanks."

We started walking. The sun had set, and the horizon was pink and pastel blue. The sky was vast. "I've been thinking," she started.

"I guessed."

"I think we need to pin down the things we know. Right? The things we know for sure. Line them up, and then see what that says to us."

I nodded. "Okay, that sounds good."

"So what do we know?" She'd had her hands in her pockets, but now she pulled them out and made a gesture, like she was setting out the things we knew in front of her. "We know that Nelson and his cousins were murdered by more than one professional. So that is our firm starting point."

"Okay."

"We know that whoever organized the hit wanted the money but not the dope. And we know that that person also took Maria. Okay?"

"That is all good, solid reasoning."

She stopped dead and I turned to face her. "So, at this point, we can say that we know that the person who took Maria is Mick, so by irresistible extension, we know that Mick killed Nelson." She held up her hand. "Wait! I know what you're going to say. Mick was with Jenny. I'll come back to that. For now, my reasoning is sound."

I shrugged. "Okay."

We started walking again. The smell of char-grilled steak wafted to us on the evening air along with the strains of the Eagles' "Tequila Sunrise." For just a moment, I felt like life didn't get much better than this. She continued reasoning.

"What else do we know?"

We had reached Big Vern's, and I held the door open for her to go in. She walked through, talking. "We know that Mick changed his name and came to Shamrock with Maria in his dream car. We know he left by an eccentric route that led west instead of south, and we know they were both killed in a very secluded spot in the Palo Duro Canyon."

She paused to give the waitress our order, which was two sixteen-ounce rib eye steaks with french fries and two beers. The waitress went away, and Dehan said, "I'm nearly done."

"You're doing fine."

"We know that the first person to point us unequivocally toward Mick was Pro. We know Pro wanted Mick found. And we know that as soon as Pro heard we had come here, he came running to discover what we'd found. Those are the things we know for sure. The question now is, what do they say to us?"

The beers came. I sipped and said, "Well, why don't you talk me through what they say to you?"

That was what she was hoping I'd say and pulled her chair in and leaned forward, "Right. The question that leaps out at me as the most relevant is, why would Pro want to know something he already knew?"

"Where Mick was?"

"Exactly. The only possible answer, and the simplest, is that he didn't know. Which means one thing—he did not kill Mick with his own hands. And accepting that, it strikes at the essence of this whole case."

I frowned, intrigued. "Explain that to me."

"From the very start, everywhere you look, there is the suggestion of somebody who was there, killed, and then vanished without leaving a trace. You mentioned it yourself. So here is how I think it works." She pushed up her sleeves. "The Bronx has a power vacuum. The Triads, the Sureños, and the Mob all want in, but Nelson is holding the high ground. At the same time, for the past year, Mick has been wanting to get out because things are getting too hot for him. So he and Pro make a deal."

I nodded. "I like this, Dehan."

Her cheeks colored, but she acted like she hadn't heard.

"Here's the deal. Mick, for a fee from each, informs both the Triad and the Jersey Mob of when Nelson's game is, when he's going to have all his takings from the rackets in the house. He arranges with each of them to turn up and eliminate Nelson, but he is going to go in first, do the job, and take the money.

"But Mick isn't stupid. He arranges an alibi for himself with Jennifer, and instead, as we discussed before, sends in Kirk with a couple of hit men to do the job for him and take the money and Maria to his place later."

"Why does Pro want Mick to do the hit first, before the Triads and the Mob turn up?"

She grinned and pointed at me. "Ha! That had me going, but when you think about it, it makes sense. Pro is a gangster, like Mick. And here is the sweet deal. The Mob and the Triads pay Mick into his bank, and Pro gets a cool half million in cash from Nelson. Everybody's happy. Plus, as a result, war breaks out between the Triads, the Mexicans, and the Mob. How is that an advantage to Pro? Well, ask yourself, how's that going to play out? Simple, the Triads are out of their territory, so they will withdraw licking their wounds, leaving the Mob and the Mexicans. The Mexicans are on their home turf, but they are disorganized and haven't got the resources or the experience of the Mob. So they'll end up running the show but paying tribute to Vincenzo through Pro. Everybody wins and Pro makes a cool half million for his personal retirement fund."

"I'm impressed. So explain to me what we found today out in the canyon."

"It comes together nicely. Pro and Mick have arranged beforehand that they will hand over the money at the Palo Duro Canyon, on his way to Mexico. Seen like that, Mick's drive to the canyon is not a detour from his journey south, but an extension of his journey west."

"Good."

"Naturally Pro cannot be directly implicated in this, so he sends a guy to collect the money for him. Mick, being Mick, explains to the guy that he can't give it to him, because he has banked it and sent it to Belize, and by the way he can kiss his sweet Irish ass. The guy shoots Mick and Maria. But before he dies, Mick shoots the guy, and ten years of rain and heat and coyotes and rats have done the rest."

She paused and took a long pull on her beer. She was going to wipe the foam from her lip with the back of her hand but stopped and used a napkin. Then grinned. "Naturally, when Pro heard that you had driven out here of all places, he had to come and see what you'd found."

I thought about it for a while. The steaks came and we ordered two more beers. "So how do we prove this?"

She shook her head. "We have to hand it over to the Feds. There are two states and two countries involved. We need a thorough search of the canyon, searching for bones, weapons, clothes—anything that will show that Mick, Maria, and a third party were there. Because you can guarantee that the car isn't registered to Mick. The bones and dental records will have to be analyzed. The evidence is going to be all forensic, and we will be very lucky to be able to tie Pro into it. All we've got there is conjecture."

I ate half my steak in silence, thinking. Then I said, "It works for you?"

She narrowed her eyes at me. "It doesn't work for you?"

"I think it's a superb piece of reasoning. I can't fault it. It's a hell of a piece of work. I'm just asking if your gut tells you you're satisfied with it."

She nodded.

"Good. Then tomorrow I'll talk to the sheriff, and we'll hand the case over to the bureau." I raised my glass to her. "*Slánta!*"

When we'd finished eating, I called the waitress over and asked her for a bottle of tequila, some lemon, and some salt. We kept it quiet, we didn't question anybody's Irishness, but we laughed a lot and got pretty silly. We staggered back to the motel at about eleven, softly singing old Bing Crosby songs about not being fenced in, and said good night at her door. We had a moment of silence when I held out my fist, and she punched it gently and said, "Detective John Stone, you are cooler'n all git out, and that ain't no lie!"

I said, "Good night, pardner."

And went quickly to my room.

Next day we both had mild hangovers, so we didn't talk much. I asked her if she would take care of the statement to the Armstrong County sheriff, and I took the SUV back up to Ted in Texola. I stood watching him while he inspected it, muttering to himself about insurance and lost vee-hickles. As I listened to him, I remembered the way he'd been talking last time I saw him. Something that had crossed my mind then began nagging at me again, so I said to him, suddenly, "So she never brought it back, huh?"

"Puts yer premium right up, when you gotta claim fer a whole SUV."

"Did she pay you extra for driving her back?"

"Can't complain on the score. She was generous enough with her money. But she was plumb crazy. Hundred bucks seem fair to you, mister?"

I realized he was talking about my rental, and I gave him a hundred and ten. He seemed happy. I asked him, "Was it just the once, or has it happened since?"

He scratched his head under his baseball cap and looked like he'd never really thought about it like that before. "No, just the once. But that's enough, ain'it?"

"Once is enough. What was that, ten years ago?"

"Got to be all of ten year, now."

"Pretty little thing."

"Cute as a button."

"Mexican."

"I'd say so, but she talked funny, like you."

"Bronx, New York."

"Guess so."

I slapped him on the shoulder. "Thanks, Ted, you take it easy."

I could see the Jaguar approaching through the heat haze along the road. Ted was staring at me, frowning. Dehan pulled up onto the dirt, and I walked over. As I opened the passenger door, he called out to me, "Say! How did you know all that?"

I waved, gave him the thumbs-up, and climbed into the car. And we took off back east.

Twenty-Three

NEW YORK FELT CRAMPED and overcrowded after the vast expanses of the Panhandle. The city contained a third of the entire population of the state of Texas, and right then, crawling down Simpson Street toward Dehan's apartment, it felt like they were all there, on that street, at the same time.

She'd had the last shift driving, and I could see from her eyes that she was exhausted. So I dropped her off and told her I'd give her a call in the morning. She punched me gently on the shoulder and said, "It's been fun. We should do it again."

I felt pretty tired myself, but there were a couple of things I needed to take care of before I collapsed. So I threaded my way onto the Bruckner Expressway and headed for the precinct.

It was approaching midday as I climbed the stairs and stepped into the captain's office. We stared at each other a moment without speaking. Then I closed the door and sat down. I didn't like the woman, but that didn't make what I had to do any easier.

"I'm sorry, Jennifer. We found Mick's car and the remains of two bodies in it. The ME will confirm through dental records, but I don't think there can be any doubt that these are the bodies of Mick Harragan and Maria Garcia."

Her face clenched for a moment, and her eyes flooded. She sat looking out of the window, chewing her lip. I gave her a moment, then said, "The case will have to go to the Feds now. The sheriffs of Wheeler and Armstrong are both making reports, and I will have to do the same. This has to be a federal case now."

I let that sink in, and after a moment, she nodded. "I have no axe to grind with you, Jennifer. I am not coming after you. As far as I am concerned, you are guilty of no more than an indiscretion and turning a blind eye. I think that disgraces you, and it makes you unfit for your office, but I will be satisfied if you resign, and what I know need go no further."

She stared down at her hands. "I suppose I ought to thank you."

"Don't thank me. Just level with me on one thing. You know me. You know I will get there in the end, and it's better you are honest with me now."

She finally met my eye and asked, "What do you want to know?"

"Did you replace Mick with the Mob? Are you feeding Morry Levy with information?"

She frowned and shook her head. "No, John. What I did with Mick ten years ago was wrong. But I am not a bent cop, and you are welcome to investigate me. I have nothing to hide."

"Okay." I stood. At the door, I said, "Jennifer, because you turned a blind eye, a lot of people suffered and died—people who shouldn't have, people who didn't deserve to. You have to go."

I was about ready to go home and sleep for twelve hours, but there was one more thing I had to do. I went down, dropped into my chair, and pulled out the cold case archive, the two cardboard boxes that now lived under my desk. I searched through them until I found the Sam Bernstein case. It was a very thin file. I leafed through it and studied it for half an hour; then I clipped it as an annex to the Nelson Hernandez case.

After that I drove up to Morris Park, to the ME's office. I found Lynda poring over the body of somebody who had stopped being anybody and was now a Caucasian male in his mid to late thirties. She glanced at me over her mask and said in a muffled voice, "John. You should have called."

"I would've if I could've, but I couldn't so I didn't."

She sighed and came over to where I was standing by the door. She removed her mask and revealed a smile. "You look terrible."

"Too much steak and beer."

"What can I do for you?"

I gave her my cell and said, "It's urgent. In fact, it's very urgent. Print the last six photographs and check them against Mick Harragan's dental records. They'll be in the NYPD database for the 43rd precinct. I know I'm asking a lot, but you need to give this top priority. I have maybe a few hours before I lose control of the case." I made a face to show that I couldn't say what I wanted to say, and added, "That would be a bad thing."

She understood and took my phone over to the printer.

When she handed it back, I called José.

"What?"

"José, can you talk?"

"Yuh."

"Did your sister have dental insurance?"

He was silent for a moment, then said, "Yeah, we all did. We used to go regular, man, every six months to have our teeth whitened in time for our Christmas and summer holidays in

Miami. We kept the papers in the fockin' oak dresser in the fockin' library."

"Shut the fuck up, José. So when you had dental work, how did you pay?"

"When we had it, like never, we paid cash."

"Thanks."

I hung up. I sat thinking for a long while. Eventually Lynda came back. She handed me a file and said, "This is an unofficial preliminary report, you understand?"

"Sure. I appreciate it."

"Speaking off the record, the larger skull is almost certainly Mick's. The other skull, without dental records I can't tell you very much at all. From the pictures it seems to be the skull of a small woman."

"Thanks. It was mainly him I was interested in. But there is something else. It was a case, ten years ago, young man shot to death in the Bronx..."

She raised an eyebrow. "That narrows it down a bit."

I smiled. "Yeah, his name was Sam Bernstein. He was from Brooklyn."

She shrugged. "Ten years ago, John... What do you want to know?"

"You examined the body, and I want to know what you found."

"You must have the ME's report in the case file."

"Yeah, but what I want to know wasn't included."

She sighed. I gave her the case details, and she found it in her database. As she read it, she said, "Oh, I vaguely remember this case. It was a bit unusual. His mother identified him in the end."

"Okay, now, it says he died from a gunshot wound to the head. It was a hollow tip and probably a .45 cal. The entry wound was at the back, right?" She was nodding as she looked at the screen. I shrugged and shook my head. "A hollow tip .45 at close range with the entry in the back of the head—Lynda, he had no face!"

She looked at me. "That's right. His face had been blown off. The exit wound was about the size of a large grapefruit, consistent with a .45 caliber. He had his driver's license and his ID card." She shook her head. "It's hard to remember details, John. It was ten years ago. But there were things about it that stood out. A middle-class, well-educated Jewish boy from Brooklyn alone in that part of the Bronx in the early hours of the morning. His mother was pretty hysterical, as you can imagine. She couldn't look at him, but she identified his clothes and his effects. What did you want to know?"

"When you get a case like that, where the face is so badly damaged, do you routinely make a record of the teeth?"

"Not routinely, but almost always."

"Did you in this case?"

She checked the screen. "We started to. But when the mother identified him, we didn't go ahead with it. Why?"

"How long would it take you?" She stared at me. "It is really important, Lynda. Somebody's life could be seriously at risk."

"Give me half an hour."

It took her twenty minutes. She came and found me in the corridor, drinking black water that pretended to be coffee. I stood as she approached, and she handed me another thin file. "Is this official or unofficial?"

"For now, unofficial."

"The dead man is not Sam Bernstein."

I put my hand on her arm and led her over to a window where we were alone. "Lynda, in a week all of this can go into an official report, and I will hold myself solely responsible. But today, there is somebody at the bureau who cannot learn about this, you understand? And this is about to become a federal investigation. If that person learns about this, Sam Bernstein will die. For real this time."

She studied my face a moment. "Okay, John. You can count on me. I trust you'll do the right thing."

Twenty-Four

I CALLED JENNIFER AND told her I was taking a week's holiday. She seemed relieved till I told her I didn't want to see her there when I got back. Then I called Dehan. She didn't answer, but I didn't expect her to. I left her a message saying whatever plans she had for that evening to cancel them and come over to my place for a barbeque. We needed to talk.

Then I went home, showered for twenty minutes, and slept for four hours.

I was awoken by the bell. I didn't know how long it had been ringing, but it felt persistent. I got up and leaned out of the window in my shorts. Dehan was at the door holding a bottle of wine. She looked up at me and, as usual, her lack of expression was extremely expressive.

"What time is it?"

"Seven thirty. You want me to go away?"

"No."

I pulled on a pair of jeans and went down to open the door. She gave me a once-over and said, "Gee, Detective Stone. You sure know how to make a girl feel special."

I pointed at the kitchen and said, "Beer. I'm going to have a shower. Make yourself at home."

When I finally came down again, it was growing dusk outside. She was sitting cross-legged on the floor going through my record collection. I opened the fridge and grabbed a beer.

"I started buying records in 1980, just before CDs came out. I still like them better. I like the way they crackle."

She was examining an original Led Zeppelin IV. "I bet you like the smell of books too."

"Yup."

"And always consult a reference book instead of checking Google."

"You nailed me."

She put the record on the turntable, worked out how to use it, and put it on low. I was pulling meat out of the fridge as the rasp of the guitar echoed into silence before the timeless voice bellowed.

"Why be virtual when you can be real, right?"

"Got it in one."

I built a small tower of paper and kindling and structured the charcoal around it in a pyramid. Then I put a match to the paper and watched the flames and the smoke start to build. We chinked bottles, drank, and sat at the garden table.

"I just know that this was not a social invitation," she said. "I can tell."

I frowned. "Not one hundred percent social, Carmen. There are a couple of things I need to talk to you about."

"About the case?"

"Indirectly."

"Where did I go wrong?"

"Don't jump to conclusions. You didn't go wrong, there just turns out to be more to it than was immediately apparent."

"What does that mean?"

"It means Sam Bernstein wasn't killed that night in the Bronx."

"Holy shit!"

"...is right."

She stood and walked out onto the lawn. The first stars were piercing the deep blue of the evening sky. After a moment, she turned to face me. "When did you find out? Did you know this back in Shamrock? This changes everything."

"I found out today. No I didn't, and I am not so sure it does."

She spread her hands and shook her head. It was like a gesture of helplessness. "How? How did you find out?"

"I took my pictures of Mick's skull to the ME. I wanted to make sure it was him. While we were talking, it struck me that dental record ID really depended a lot—" I gave a small laugh. "—on your having dental records to begin with."

"Obviously."

"A lot of the less privileged people in our society haven't got dental insurance," I went on, "and so their dental records are sketchy at best or nonexistent. Sam would have known that."

"What's your point?"

I was thoughtful for a bit, watching the flames in the barbeque, feeling their heat reaching my face in the evening air.

"I have never been really comfortable with Sam's murder. The timing was just too much of a coincidence. A gunshot wound to the head. Probably a .45. A .45 was what Sam took from his father's trunk. When I looked closer at the details of the wound, the entry was at the back of the skull, the exit through the front." I shook my head, "Not just an execution, but an execution designed to disfigure." We stared at each other a moment as she assimilated the implications. "And let's face it, what mother is going to examine her son's face in that condition? She's going to close her eyes and look away. She is going to see his clothes, his personal effects, and she is going to say it's him. And who is going to question that? We have his ID papers. The cops are going to think, this middle-class schmuck was at Hunts Point at two a.m., probably looking for a whore, and he got mugged. What did he expect?"

"So you're saying Sam killed some kid?"

I shrugged. "Looks that way to me."

"So who did Jennifer and Mick talk to?"

I smiled. "Sam."

"Shit. Why? What was he trying to do?"

"I don't know."

"Have you told the Feds?"

"I haven't told anybody yet except the ME and you. And I asked Lynda to keep quiet about it till I am ready. I'm asking you the same thing."

"I got to tell you, I am lost."

I sighed and nodded. "I think that was the idea."

"What are you going to do?"

"I'm going to take a few days off. Go away."

"Where?"

I smiled. "I think I'll put some flowers in my hair and go to San Francisco. I hear summertime will be a love-in there."

"You want me to come with you?"

I smiled, my gaze lost in the flames.

"Where I'm going, you can't follow. What I've got to do, you can't be any part of, Dehan. But we'll always have Shamrock."

"Asshole."

The coals had burned down, and I stood to put the steaks on the grill. I threw on a handful of fresh thyme first and then laid on the oiled steaks as the flames leapt and licked at the meat. The haunting strains of a mandolin trailed out onto the evening air.

Dehan asked me, "Is Maria Garcia dead?"

I poured the rich wine, red like dense blood, into the two glasses. The intense orange of the fire glowed within it like a living thing. "Oh yes." I handed her a glass. "There can be no doubt about that at all. Maria Garcia is dead."

"Who killed her?"

I stared into her black eyes. She knew what I was going to say, but she needed to hear me say it.

"Sam Bernstein."

Twenty-FIVE

I TOUCHED DOWN IN SAN Francisco at ten in the morning and picked up my hire car at the Hertz desk. I treated myself to a Mustang Cabrio convertible and took it easy to my hotel on Taylor Street, via the Sierra Point Parkway.

I checked in, had a shower, and changed my clothes, then settled down to do some research. There are a lot of universities in and around San Francisco. It took a lot of old-fashioned, dinosaur-style, tedious looking up lists and making phone calls, and progress was slow. At midday I went for a walk, found some food, and took it back to my room, where I continued making lists, making phone calls, and crossing entries off my lists. It was like a pulse, like the rhythm of life: accumulate, eliminate, accumulate more, eliminate more.

I get deep like that sometimes. Dehan would approve.

By the time I fell into bed that night, I felt I had done about all I could do over the phone. So the next morning, after coffee and croissants, I took my Mustang and drove across the bay, via the Dwight Eisenhower Highway, to Berkeley. I got lost for a bit, enjoying the feeling of being at large in a cool, hip city, and finally wound up at Tolman Hall and the psychology department. I found my way to the student office and finally tracked down Tania Goodman, whom I had spoken to on the phone the day before.

She was sweet, and that always helps.

I took her aside, told her who I was and that I was there in an unofficial capacity on behalf of a friend. She glanced at her watch, said she was about to grab some coffee, and would I like to join her? I said I would. We strolled down to the cafeteria and eventually sat. She smiled at me, and I thought that she was pretty, in a neurotic sort of way. She had short blonde hair and very blue eyes that had a tendency to stare while she grinned.

"I am looking for a woman who would have moved out here about ten years ago, as a student. She lost touch with her mother and her brother, who was only ten at the time. Now the mother is very sick, and the boy feels his sister should know. In case she wants to come back and see her..." I shrugged, allowing the implication to sit there between us.

"That is so sad. You think she came here, to Berkeley?"

"It's probable. She was keen and very bright, and she very interested in psychology. I've tried to access lists of old alumni online, but it isn't easy."

She frowned. "Sure. I can tell you if she studied here. But I can't give you any contact information." I told her I understood that. "What is her name?"

"Maria Garcia."

She giggled. "Do you know how many John Smiths we get in a year? Well, we get that many Maria Garcias too. I'll have a look for you though."

She took me back to her computer terminal, and I sat next to her while she rattled at the keyboard and entered the filters into the database. After a while she said, "We had four Maria Garcias join the psychology undergraduate program in 2008. One of them was from Mexico City, two were from San Francisco. One of them was from LA."

She turned and watched me chew my lip. She must have liked me because she was very patient and tried 2009 too, but with no joy. Finally she said, "Look, I have to get back to work. I shouldn't do this, but one of the students you just viewed wound up doing her PhD here and now works as a lecturer in child psychology. It's a long shot, but if your Maria was here at that time, they might have known each other."

I thanked her and she told me where the lecturer had her office. She had since married and was now Maria Chandler.

I got lost again among the corridors but eventually found her door. I knocked and a voice told me to come in. It was a small office with a window and lots of filing cabinets. There was a woman with disorganized dark hair sitting behind the desk, who must have been in her midthirties. There was a bald man in chinos, and a woman with short, sandy hair and large glasses. They were both of a similar age, and they were sitting in armchairs, also drinking coffee. They all looked at me, and I felt like I was interrupting a break. I didn't really care and said, "Maria Chandler?"

The woman behind the desk said, "That's me."

"I wonder if you could spare me five minutes of your time. It is actually quite serious."

The man and the woman went to rise, but Maria said, "No, hang on." And to me, "What's it about?"

"I am a police detective from New York, and I am trying to trace somebody, unofficially, because they may be in danger."

The guy said, "Whoa!" and Maria raised an eyebrow at me. I pulled out my badge and handed it over to her. While she examined it, I looked at the other two and said, "Were you all students here back in 2008?"

The girl said, "Yes."

"Then you might be able to help." I looked at Maria again and made a question with my face. She said, "Why don't you tell us, briefly, what this is about and we'll take it from there."

I gave them the bones: that it was a cold case, that Maria Garcia had gone missing, that a couple of the people involved had shown up dead, and that we had reason to believe that Maria's life might be at risk. The woman behind the desk said, "Maria Garcia? That's my name."

I smiled. "That's why I'm here, talking to you."

"But I'm not from the Bronx..."

"I know that. There were four Maria Garcias in your year. None of them was from New York. But it's possible that she changed her name. She was escaping from a very violent past, where she had been exploited and abused, so she may have changed her identity."

The idea that she had been exploited and abused must have appealed to their sensibilities because their demeanor changed and they all frowned in thought at the same time. The woman with the glasses said, "You know who? That girl. She was shy. She said she was from Michigan." The guy had started nodding. She went on, "But she had that 'noo yoik' kind of accent? She used to say 'caw-fee' instead of coffee? I never really believed that she was from Michigan. What was her name?"

The guy said, "Mary. Her name was Mary. Mary..." He sighed and looked at Maria, who was staring back at him. She said, suddenly, "Browne, with an *e*. Mary Browne. That's right, she said she was from Michigan. What did this girl look like, Detective?"

I was still standing. They hadn't invited me to sit down, but I leaned my back against the door and said, "I haven't got a picture, but by all accounts she was pretty. She was of Mexican origin, short, dark hair, olive skin, dark eyes..."

Maria said, "This girl wasn't pretty." The girl with the glasses said, "Hmmmm..." like she didn't agree. "Could have been. Lovely eyes." The guy said, "She just didn't look after herself. She looked drawn and tired all the time, but she was quite cute. Lovely body. She was married. I remember she was married."

"Hence Browne."

"There you have it. Hence the Browne."

I interrupted. "Is there any way I can find out what happened to her? When she graduated, did she go on to further study, did she go into clinical practice..."

Maria picked up the phone. "Tania, it's Maria Chandler. Can you look up something for me and call me straight back? Mary Browne, graduated from here probably in 2012. I need to contact her."

They looked at me while we waited, and the guy said suddenly, "So that kind of thing really happens, huh?"

"Yeah, it happens." I smiled. "I never yet arrested anybody for being a Communist, but I lost count of the people I arrested for homicide."

That caused an uncomfortable silence which I smiled through until the phone rang. I figured Dehan would have been proud of me. Maria scrawled something down on a piece of paper and handed it to me.

"We are not all left-wing hippies, Detective. And we don't all think you are pigs. Mary Browne graduated with honors in 2012. She then went into training as a clinical psychologist, specializing in child psychology and PTSD. The contact information here is nothing more than you could have got from the Yellow Pages, so I am not giving you any private information."

I thanked them and left. I found my way back to my car and sat in the sun thinking about what I had learned. Her practice was on Market Street, back where I had come from, a stone's throw from my hotel. Was it her? Was it Maria Garcia, now Mary Browne, clinical psychologist from Berkeley, originally from Hunts Point in the Bronx? Or was she a completely different person, originally from Michigan?

I fired up the Mustang and cruised back across the bay, watching the sun explode in a trillion manic shards of light across the water, while I drummed on the steering wheel and asked myself, what now, John Stone, what now?

Twenty-Six

I PARKED OUTSIDE WESTFIELD on Market Street and dodged across the road. Her building was one of those nice old stone buildings from the turn of the nineteenth century. Her clinic was on the fifth floor. There was a comfortable waiting room with black leather armchairs and lots of magazines, and a comfortable woman with a comfortable smile sitting behind a reception desk.

I was trying to look neurotic. That's supposed to be easy for New Yorkers. But I wasn't sure what to do so, so I just acted naturally and it seemed to work.

"I'd like to make an appointment to see Dr. Mary Browne."

She tapped into her computer and said, "When would you like to see her?"

"As soon as possible. Can it be today?"

She looked at me like I was magic. Maybe she thought I was using Jungian synchronicity. I smiled. She said, "Well, if you don't mind waiting, she has a cancellation in half an hour! May I have your name?"

"That's superb. John Stone."

"Have you insurance?"

"No."

"Then that will be seventy dollars for the hour."

I almost told her that it was cheaper, and healthier, than a Bronx hooker, but decided against it. I sat and read an article about the Larsen Ice Shelf in the Antarctic, and just as I was coming to the good bit, I heard my name being called.

I stepped into her room and closed the door behind me. There was a window that looked out over Market Street. I could see my car outside Westfield. The carpet was gray, and she had a beige calico sofa and two beige calico armchairs arranged around a coffee table. She didn't get up. She sat and watched me.

I was aware of a strange thrill of excitement but tried to ignore it.

She was lovely. Not beautiful—she was also beautiful—but more than that she was lovely. She was about thirty-one or two. Her hair was dark and cut to shoulder-length in a rather old-fashioned style. Her eyes were large and a deep brown. She was smiling. Her expression was humorous but above all kind.

"Are you Dr. Mary Browne?"

"Yes. And you are John Stone." I sat down. "What seems to be the problem, John? Marylyn said you wanted to see me as soon as possible."

I stared at her. I had somehow imagined that once I saw her I would know. But I had no idea whether this was her or not. I said, "Your accent." I smiled. "I'm a New Yorker, from the Bronx. Do I detect a trace of New York there?"

Her eyes glistened. "That's what we call evasion. You have an hour, John, and we want to use it. Time is precious. You didn't want to see me about my accent. So, what's troubling you?"

"I'm a cop. But I have developed a real fear of violence. I can't watch it on TV or on the news, and if there's a chance of encountering it on the job, I start shaking, my palms go sweaty, I feel sick..."

She looked serious and made a note in her pad.

"When did you start getting these reactions?"

"About two weeks ago."

"Can you think of anything that happened two weeks ago that might have triggered these reactions?"

I was making it up as I went along, and I know the cardinal rule when lying is stick to the truth in every detail you possibly can. So I said, "Only thing I can think of is I was assigned to head up a cold cases team. Just me and one other detective."

"Have you had any violent experiences since you started?"

I watched her carefully. "I witnessed a murder. An ex-cop called Kirk."

She looked up at me and met my eye. She had absolutely no expression on her face. "Kirk. What happened?"

"It was a UPS deliveryman. He went up to his front door and shot him."

She waited. I wasn't sure what else to say. "To you, John. What happened to you?"

For a moment I wasn't sure what she meant. Then I said, "Oh! Well, like I said, I started shaking and sweating. Luckily my partner was there, and she was able to catch the guy and make the arrest."

"And since then?"

"Nothing really."

"This is a new partner?"

"Yeah. She was assigned to me for the cold cases."

"You get on well?" She looked up and smiled as she asked it. I smiled back.

"Yeah. Nobody else can stand her, but we get on really well."

She grinned and pointed at me with her pen. "I can see it on your face. You really light up when you think of her."

I waved a hand at her. "Nah! She's a smart cookie. An intelligent woman. I know she's got my back."

She grinned and made a few notes.

"How long have you had feelings for her?"

"Come on!" I laughed. "She's my partner. She's like a pal. Could be a guy. Got a mouth on her you could grow mushrooms in. No way."

She raised an eyebrow. "Really? It's an issue you should address, John."

I made a "Pfff!" sound.

"So there have been no other violent incidents?"

"Well, just the one. We made an arrest. It was a drugs bust at... Well, doesn't matter where. It was a drugs bust. Two Mexican guys got shot. We arrested another two..." The memory was coming back real vivid. "I saw Carlitos was aiming his gun right at her. And his pal was aiming at me. And it was weird because I disarmed Carlitos, and she kind of dodged behind my back and disarmed the guy who was going to shoot me..."

She was staring hard at me. Again she had no expression at all on her face. After a moment she said, "And how did that affect you?"

For a moment, I faltered. "I...uh... It shook me up."

"Thinking that she risked her life for you?"

"I guess..."

"Or thinking that you risked your life for her?"

"Um, I hadn't thought about it."

"I'm aware of that, John. That's why I am suggesting you *should* think about it." She checked her notes. "So, in the last two weeks these are the only times when you have confronted violence. How long ago were they?"

"They were both within a day of each other, right back in the beginning."

She nodded a while, then said, "So, what I'm a bit confused about, John, is how do you know you are having these bad reactions, if those are the only times you have been exposed to violence?"

I made a mental note. Next time I was going to bullshit a psychologist, I should prepare my story. I made up something about my dreams, and she wanted to know if I had been dreaming about Dehan. I told her I hadn't. The hour was really dragging. In the end I said to her, "You know, Doc, for cops it's really important to be able to rely on your partner without having weird, romantic, sexual kind of shit going on."

"Why do you call it shit? Is that how you see it?" I was spared having to answer because she looked at the clock on the wall and said, "It is also very important for human being to be able to acknowledge their true feelings."

On my way out, I asked Marylyn the receptionist, for future reference, what their latest slot was. She said it was from five to six p.m.

I drove back to the hotel, had some lunch, and threw myself on my bed to stare at the ceiling for a while. I had four hours to kill. My phone pinged. It was a WhatsApp message from Dehan.

How's it hangin' partner?
I typed,

I just told a psychoanalyst I am in love with you.

Fuck you

Thank you. I hoped you would say that

At five thirty I went down, drove back to Market Street, and parked once more outside Westfield. I put the soft top up, closed the windows, and waited.

Twenty-SEVEN

SHE CAME OUT AT ABOUT six fifteen and stood on the sidewalk, peering up to her right, like she was waiting for somebody. I watched her for about five minutes, wondering if it was her, if she was that Maria Garcia that Nelson and Mick and Sam had all fallen for in their own, peculiar ways. If she was, I could see why. She wasn't my style, but there was something enchanting and captivating about her—a mix of vulnerability, intelligence and strength that was rare and beautiful.

I saw her smile, and a moment later a burgundy Range Rover pulled up with its hazards on. She skipped around to the passenger door and climbed in, saying something and laughing. I caught a glimpse of the driver, but it was hard to make anything out.

They pulled away. I let them get ahead of me and began to follow. Whoever it was drove assertively, bordering on aggressive. He weaved his way through the traffic, not so much settling into its flow as driving through it to get where he wanted to be. He led me back to the Dwight Eisenhower Highway and across the bay again. I followed him onto the I-80 along the coast, then onto Ashby Avenue and into South Berkeley. Next thing we were driving down quiet, leafy streets among cute, detached houses with front and back gardens that probably came with a price tag of between one and a half and two million bucks.

They turned into Blake Street, and I slowed right down to give them a chance to park and get out. After thirty seconds or a minute, I turned in after them and drove slowly past. It was a double-fronted, gabled affair that looked as though it might have been built in the thirties. It had a cute wooden arch with a rose bush growing over it that led to the front door. I just caught a glimpse of her bending down to hug a couple of kids as he held the door open. The kids were about four or five. He was about thirty-two and dark.

I drove on by.

I drove slowly, drumming a tattoo on the steering wheel as I chewed my lip and thought. The roads were empty, and dusk was creeping across the sky. I noticed absently in my mirror that there was a dark blue Audi 8 some distance behind me. Some people play with worry beads, some people have a special pen for signing contracts, others have a St. Christopher in their car. I have a stupid notion that bad guys always drive black or dark blue Audis. It is my thing. So I turned right into McGee Avenue at the end of the road and waited for him at the junction with Dwight Way, like I wasn't sure which way to go. He came up behind me, but I couldn't see his face because his windows were tinted. I turned right into Dwight, and he followed. So I turned right again into Grant, and as he followed again, I turned right once more into Blake again and stopped. I got out and walked back toward him as he turned in behind me. I made a motion he should wind down his window. Instead he pulled out past me and drove away at speed.

I got back in my car and returned to my hotel.

I had a light supper. While I was eating, my mind was racing. It was obvious to me who was in the Audi. What was troubling me was, when did they pick me up? Had they been with me when I went into Mary Browne's clinic? Did they know who I'd been tailing? I probed back with my mind. I was pretty sure that I would have noticed a dark Audi tailing me.

Also, logic suggested they had not been with me very long—or at least they did not know who I had been tailing, because they had continued past her house, following me, not who I was following.

That night I slept fitfully. By six a.m. I had to get up, though I felt more tired than when I'd gone to bed. I had a shower and called room service for coffee and croissants. I was out by eight. It was a bright, fresh morning with the first hints of autumn in the air. I stood in the doorway of the hotel scanning the road left and right. Everybody seemed to be moving. There was nobody staring in a shop window, loitering reading the morning paper or waiting on the corner for a cab. So I moved into the crowd and took a long, winding, circuitous route to Market Street. I was pretty sure by the time I got there, I had not been followed.

I went up to the fifth floor and pushed into the clinic. Marylyn looked surprised to see me but forced herself to smile.

"Mr. Stone, back so soon? I didn't think we'd made an appointment..."

I shook my head. "We didn't, but this is an emergency. I am having a crisis, and I need to see the doctor right away. Or I might do something crazy."

"But she isn't in yet..."

"I'll wait."

"But she has a nine o'clock, Mr. Stone..."

I shook my head again, more insistently, "I'm telling you. I need to see her now, or I'm going to jump out of a window or do something crazy. I mean it."

She stared at me. I tried to look crazy. She picked up the phone. After a moment, she said, "Mary? It's Mr. Stone from yesterday. He is very insistent that he must see you straight away…"

"Tell her I'll do something crazy."

She listened for a moment, then hung up.

"She is just arriving. You can have fifteen minutes. After that you *must* make an appointment."

As she was speaking, the door opened behind me and Mary Browne came in. She gave me a look like I was a naughty boy and said, "Come on in."

I followed her into the consulting room and closed the door. I dropped into a chair while she took off her coat and hung it up.

"What is all this about, John?"

"I have this recurring nightmare."

"We have fifteen minutes."

"I know, so don't interrupt me. This could be important for you." I pointed at her chair. "Sit down. It goes like this. I'm in the Bronx. You know the Bronx?"

She shook her head and sat, holding a notepad and a pen. I shrugged.

"I'm in the Bronx. It's nighttime. Maybe two in the morning. I am like a ghost. I have no substance. You know what I mean? Like an invisible eye floating in the air. And there are two scenes being played out. And I can see them both happening simultaneously. You still with me?"

She nodded. She hadn't written anything down yet.

"One scene is in the street. There's a young kid, maybe twenty, twenty-one. He's Jewish. He's kind of lost, but he's lost in a rage. He has a revolver. It's a pearl-handled revolver that his father had."

I paused, watching her. There was no reaction, no expression. I went on.

"So this boy is about to do something very bad. He is about to kill somebody. Meanwhile, I am also aware of a girl, a very pretty young Mexican girl. Her name is Maria—Maria Garcia."

I stared at her a long time, waiting for some kind of reaction. There was nothing. Nothing at all.

"Maria is at a party. More than a party, really, it's a poker game. There are five guys there. I even know their names. Nelson Hernandez, Dickson Rodriguez, Evandro Perez, José Perez, and Geronimo Peralta. They are drinking beer, whiskey, eating potato chips and peanuts. They are all very cruel to Maria. They abuse her, they prostitute her. Especially, they prostitute her to one man. An Irishman. He's a bent cop. His name is Mick. Mick Harragan."

Still she stared at me, like she was in a trance.

"That night, at almost exactly the same time, this young Jewish kid will shoot a young Latino kid in the head, and Nelson and his four cousins will get murdered. This is my recurring nightmare, Dr. Browne. What can you tell me about that?"

She blinked and took a deep breath. She laid her pad and her pen down on the table in front of her and said, "What do you want, Mr. Stone? You are not neurotic, you do not suffer panic attacks, and you do not have recurring nightmares. So why don't you just tell me what you want?"

I took out my badge and slid it across the table. She looked at it, but she didn't touch it. "I know it's you, Maria. I am not here in an official capacity. I'm here as a friend. I want to help you. Pro is looking for you. I don't know why. I know most of it, but I don't know why Pro wants you. But if you level with me, I can help you.

"José needs you. He misses you, and so does your mother."

At the mention of José, her face changed, but not in any way you could put your finger on. Maybe it froze a bit; maybe her eyes lost focus a bit. She didn't answer for a few moments, and then she sighed deeply and said, "I am sorry, Mr. Stone. You have made a mistake. I have nothing to say to you, and you are wasting your time. I have no idea what you are talking about."

I stepped out into the morning sunshine completely nonplussed. I had played my best card, and she had been too cool and too smart for me. She had outplayed me every step of the way. All I had managed was to consolidate my own certainty that she was in fact Maria Garcia. But I had proved nothing and, in the end, achieved nothing.

It dawned on me slowly as I walked that I was watching a deep blue Audi 8 moving through the traffic ahead of me. I told myself there must be a million dark blue Audis in San Francisco. I looked back. I scanned the road. I couldn't see a single other Audi.

I swore violently. I had no idea what to do next.

Twenty-EIGHT

I HUNG AROUND, READING papers and drinking coffee until lunchtime, waiting to see if the Audi came back. It didn't. But all the while I was aware that what I had was not a plan. It wasn't even a strategy. I was just being reactive to an unknown situation, and that can only lead to one place. Disaster.

I couldn't spend the rest of my life sitting on the sidewalk outside her office or her house, waiting for Pro and Vito to show up so I could protect her from them. Neither would she let me talk to her. I needed to regroup and think about my options. So I went back to the hotel, had some lunch, and then went and lay on the bed to think things through.

I was pretty sure Pro was acting on his own with Vito. Vincenzo would not be a part of this for reasons that were obvious to me. It was also clear that he would not act in broad daylight on Market Street. The days when the Mob had the kind of power that would allow them to do that sort of thing were long gone. That meant that his appearance the previous evening in Berkeley and today on Market Street were part of his reconnaissance. And that led me irresistibly to one conclusion. He was preparing to strike, and he would strike without delay—and that meant tonight.

I thought of Maria—Mary Browne—sitting in her consulting room listening to me talk. I thought of her kind, humane face, of her courage. I thought of her greeting her children in the doorway, and the shadowy figure of her husband, and I began to structure in my mind the steps I had to take.

The only sound in the room was the soft sigh of the air-con. My back, my arms, and my legs ached. I was tired. I had slept badly. The sound of the air-con was soothing. I closed my eyes to help myself concentrate. Focus.

Center my mind.

Dehan was good at that. She had impressed me in Texas with her thinking. Texas, where the sky was like a dark prairie, and the stars were like ice reflected in the surface of her aviators as we moved irresistibly down the long, straight, interminable road toward Mick's death.

I opened my eyes. The room was dark. I looked at the window. It was a dull gray square. It was dusk. I was about to swear and sit up, but a sound stopped me. I froze and listened. A gentle clunk. A keycard in the lock. A slit of light. A shadow, warped like a snake of blackness against the slit. The light died and I heard the soft click of the door closing. I could not reach my piece from where I was. In my mind I counted out the steps he would need to take to get a bead on me. Three. My form would be just visible in the dull light from the window.

I visualized, one, two, three. As he raised his weapon to take aim, I hurled myself on the floor. There was no shot. I looked up. His silhouette was moving. The communicating door between my room and the next had opened. A second figure stood in the doorway, holding a gun. I was outnumbered and unarmed. I did the only thing I could do. I roared and charged.

I collided with a body, knocking it off balance. Blindly I drove two powerful punches into it. I heard a grunt as it fell away from me. A foot on my chest hurled me against the far wall. I charged again, lashing out with my foot at where the darkness seemed blackest. I caught something, and a powerful blow glanced off my shoulder. Fingers clutched at me. I gripped back with my left hand, pile-driving punches with my right.

Then an intense light, like a laser, blinded me. I heard a *phut! phut!* and the body I was pounding sagged and slipped to the floor. I fervently thanked whatever gods provide ironic good fortune and leapt for the door. I wrenched it open and ran. My mind was running faster than I was.

I was unarmed. My piece was still on the bedside table. My car keys were in my pocket. Pro had just ordered a hit on me. That meant one thing and one thing only. He was ready to make his move on Maria. And if he wanted to eliminate me, it was for two reasons: I knew the truth, and he wanted me out of the way when he hit Maria Garcia. So my plan was get to Maria and stop Pro.

Simple.

I burst into the stairwell and took the steps a landing at a time. I crossed the lobby in Olympic gold-medal time, crashed through the doors, and vaulted into the Mustang. The tires squealed as I pulled away from the curb and hurtled along Market Street toward the bay. All the way along the Dwight Eisenhower Highway, I demonstrated the Doppler effect as horns faded in a descending note behind me. The sky was darkening to deep blue, and the first stars were appearing over the Berkeley Hills as I screamed, skidding off the Highway and onto the I-80. The traffic was heavy because of the time of day. But I blared my horn, cut people off, wove through the lanes, and never dropped below eighty.

I came off at Ashby Avenue, screamed onto Sacramento Street praying the cops would not notice me, and then burned rubber turning onto Dwight Way. I slammed on the brakes at the corner with Grant. Jumped out and ran.

I was too late. As I skidded to a halt at the corner of Grant and Blake, I saw the dark blue Audi sitting outside her house. There was a guy leaning his ass against the hood, smoking. Past him I could see into their living room. It looked like Maria and a man were sitting on the sofa, staring up at a tall gangly guy I was sure was Pro, and another whom I did not know. As I watched, the other guy pulled the drapes closed. I wondered where the kids were. I glanced at the top floor. There were no lights visible.

Next door there was an apartment block, and between her house and the block there was an alley. Two got you twenty that there was an access to the alley beyond the apartments. I put my hands in my pockets and walked past the guy sitting on the Audi like I was going somewhere. He ignored me. His fingernails were more interesting than I was.

At the end of the apartment block, there was a recess where all the trash cans were kept. Behind the cans was a wall. I hopped up and over, and I was in the alley at the back of Maria's house. I moved quietly and covered the fifty yards to her back garden without being noticed. There was a six-foot wooden fence with a door in it. I tried the door, but it was locked. I tried the fence. It was sturdy. I pulled myself up and over and grazed my chest and stomach. It hurt.

I landed softly on a well-kept lawn and crouched in the shadow of some rosebushes. I could see what I assumed was the kitchen window. There was a faint light, like a light from another room, but the kitchen was in darkness. Next to the window there was a door. The way it is with kitchen doors that lead out to gardens, is when you are out, they are locked. When you're home, they are unlocked. How long had the Brownes been home before Pro arrived?

I sprinted across the grass to the door and gently tried the handle. They had been home long enough to unlock the door. I pushed it open and stepped inside. There were voices, three of them. First I heard Maria's, quiet, reasonable, but with an edge of obstinacy.

"I am afraid you have made a mistake. I have no idea what you are talking about."

The same litany she had offered me. Probably the litany she had been rehearsing for the last ten years. Then I heard a man. His voice was educated, intelligent.

"Look, it must be obvious to you that you have made a mistake somewhere along the line. Whoever these people are you are searching for..."

Then there was a loud slap and a stifled scream from Maria. Then Pro's unmistakable voice.

"Do I *look* stupid? I may look many things. I am not beautiful. Hey, Antonio, am I beautiful? I don't think so. But I am not *stupid* either. So, please, don't insult my intelligence. A man like me gets very upset when you insult his intelligence..."

I was going to have to do something fast, and I had absolutely no idea what. I slipped into the hallway and inched toward the open door of the living room, where soft light was spilling out onto the parquet floor. I had no weapon, and I was up against two armed killers. I turned and slipped back into the kitchen. I had seen a block by the cooker with a collection of

Sabatier knives. That would have to do. In my mind was also the fact that there was a man outside, and the second killer in my room would be on his way. I was short of time.

I was short of everything.

I made to return to the living room, armed with a large knife, and saw Antonio in the doorway covering me with a Desert Eagle.

"Whatcha planning to do with the knife, cop? I hope you wasn't planning to hurt anybody with it."

"No," I said. "I thought I'd peel some onions for the Bolognese sauce."

He edged around and flicked his gun toward the living room. "Come on, wise guy. Drop the blade and move."

Pro watched me come in with real disappointment on his face. He looked disgusted. "You know? I really trusted you, Stone. I thought we had understood each other."

I glanced down at Maria and her husband. They were watching me impassively. His right cheek was inflamed, and his eyes were watering. Maria said, "What the hell are you doing here?" I ignored her and eyed Pro.

"I don't know why, Pro. I told you from the start that I don't work for you."

He gestured to a chair. "Sit down and shut up. You are a real disappointment to me."

I moved to the chair and sat. "You're making a mistake with these people. Maria Garcia is dead. So are Mick and Sam. There is nobody left but you."

I sensed Maria and her husband glance at each other. Pro stared at me, and there was real rage in his eyes. He made several "W" sounds, like his own incredulity would not allow him to finish the words. Then he blurted, "What is it with you people? You look at me and you see a fuckin' moron? What? What am I? What do I look like?"

I knew he was going to launch into one of his Hollywood wise-guy acts, so I cut him short.

"Yes, Pro. I look at you and I see a fucking moron." He and Antonio both looked astonished, but I didn't give a damn and I plowed on. "We found the Mustang in Texas, in the Palo Duro Canyon. There were two skeletons in it. They have both been identified from dental records as belonging to Maria Garcia and Mick Harragan."

He shook his head. "No."

"Yes! And the money he stole from you went straight into his numbered account in Belize, where it will stay because everybody who knew the details of the account is dead."

He stared at me hard, narrowing his eyes. "Then what the fuck are you doing here, Stone? Answer me that. Following this chick, trailing her home, getting your fuckin' hotel room almost in the same fuckin' street as her clinic. What is your *fuckin'* interest in this woman?"

He was practically screaming. I looked at him, letting the contempt I felt for him show on my face. "Keep your hair on, Pro. You're like a hysterical woman. Mick's dental records were on the NYPD database. He was a cop, remember? Maria didn't have medical insurance, so her records had to be tracked down. While they did that, I followed a personal hunch that she might have come to Berkeley. I knew she had an interest in psychology. As it turned out, she never came here. This is Mary Browne. She is from Michigan, not New York.

"This morning I put her to the test in her consulting room, and she passed with flying colors." I turned to her. "You must have thought I was even crazier than I said I was."

She met my eye and spoke with no trace of humor. "I knew you were perfectly sane, and I also knew you were lying."

I looked back at Pro. "Plus, I got notification today from my partner that the dental records match Maria's. I was being thorough—you were just being stupid."

"No..."

"*Yes*" Now the way I see it, Pro, you have a simple choice. Go home and act like none of this ever happened, or keep pushing. And if you keep pushing, I am going to make damn sure you go down for Mick and Maria's murder in Texas. If you recall, they don't fuck around in Texas. And if you go down for killing a cop in that state, you go down for good." I raised my hands. "I am going to get my cell to show you the notification. Okay?"

Antonio stepped forward, training his .45 on me. Pro pulled a Sig 9 mm from under his arm and thrust it in my face.

"Do me a favor," he said, "and try something stupid."

I spoke in a weary voice, like his stupidity was exhausting me. "You're a piece of work, Pro. You know that?"

I carefully reached in my pocket and pulled out my cell. I flicked through to my WhatsApp and found Dehan. I didn't open the conversation. I left that for him to do. I handed him my phone. "That's my partner. You've met her. It's the last message from her."

He took the phone and stared at it. He frowned as he clumsily opened the message with a gun in his hand. Very calmly, I reached forward, took hold of the barrel, and levered down hard. I did it so naturally that it took them a full four seconds to realize what was happening. Pro screamed as his fingers were twisted against their joints. He was still holding it with a twisted hand as I directed the barrel at Antonio and pulled the trigger, twice.

Twenty-NINE

THE SIG WAS NOT SILENCED, and the shots rang out loud and clear. One tore through his belly. The other exploded into his chest. I didn't wait for Pro to react. I stood and smashed my elbow into his face, snarling, "Let go, Pro!"

He did and fell sprawling onto a coffee table, which collapsed under his weight. Blood was streaming from his nose, and he was making incoherent noises. I got the idea it hurt. "Get on your belly and put your hands behind your head."

"Just what I was going to suggest you do, Stone."

I raised my eyes. I might have guessed. Vito and the guy who'd been sitting with his ass on the Audi. I figured in that moment it must have been Vito who tried to shoot me in my room. But he looked down at Pro and said, "We were sitting in the car and heard the shots. You okay, boss?"

I frowned a second. Then I slapped a smile on the right side of my face and said, "Is this what you'd call an Italian standoff?"

Pro got up on one elbow. "You're funny, Stone. Deep down funny, where it ain't like funny anymore. But you're not going to shoot me, because if you do, Vito is gonna shoot you and this sweet family you care so much about." He staggered to his feet, pulling a handkerchief from his jacket to stem the flow of blood. "Drop the gun and sit down. Now, you and hubby here are going to watch while a certain little lady starts losing fingers, until somebody tells me where my *fuckin' money is*!"

The last was a scream of rage. Maria's husband put his arms around her. I shook my head. "I'll tell you what's going to happen, Pro. Vito and his pal are going to die now. And you are going to stand trial in Texas for the murders of Maria Garcia and Mick Harragan. I gave you your chance. You didn't take it."

Pro sneered, "Bullshit!"

There was a kind of "*Hunh!*" sound from the door. He turned to look. Vito's pal was sinking to his knees, and his neck looked awful floppy. Vito had a look of vague astonishment, because he was looking into Dehan's face, and as beautiful as she looked to me right then, to Vito she must have looked terrifying.

Her hands moved too fast for the eye to follow. Two blows went to his floating ribs, and as he doubled up, her elbow smashed his jaw. Then she had his head in an armlock, and she gave a little jerk, which was the last thing Vito ever experienced in this world.

Pro was looking down the barrel of his own Sig Sauer p226. I smiled at him. "Hello, Detective Dehan. If you have quite finished showing off, would you like to cuff Mr. Levy here?"

"Love to."

The next hour was spent giving vague and evasive answers to Detective Armstrong of the SFPD, who arrived on the scene after I called in the incident, and explaining repeatedly that this was now, in fact, an FBI investigation, and that Detective Dehan and I had been assisting the FBI in their inquiries when Pro and his men had invaded Mary Browne's home.

Eventually a couple of Feds, Special Agents Turner and Caruso, arrived on the scene. They confirmed what I had said and told Detective Armstrong, politely, that they would take it from here. I explained again that Mary Browne was a case of mistaken identity and that this family had nothing to do with the investigation.

Turner said, "We are only here representing the New York field office, Detective Stone. They may have more questions for you when you get back."

With that they left, taking Pro with them. The ME arrived with a couple of meat wagons and the bodies were removed, and the last sirens and flashing red and blue lights withdrew into the early fall San Francisco night. I turned to Mary Browne. "Where are your children?"

She looked me straight in the eye. "After your visit this morning, we imagined this would happen, so we sent them to stay with friends."

Her husband spoke to me for the first time, and I could see a repressed rage in his eyes. "I don't know whether to thank you or bust your head open, Detective Stone. Why couldn't you have left us alone?"

Dehan had her ass on the windowsill, and I lowered myself into a chair. I leaned my elbows on my knees and looked him in the eye.

"Sam, you are an intelligent man, but you let your anger and your passion get the better of you. Men like Pro never give up. He didn't even know that you existed, but in his mind your wife and Mick had taken what belonged to him. He's been searching for you for ten years. Sooner or later he would have found you. So you can thank me."

I turned to Mary—Maria. "I said it's over. You don't need to hide anymore. The official version is that Mick ordered Kirk to kill Nelson. It's an explanation that the authorities can live with. You can let them think that you died in Palo Duro with Mick, or you can resume your real identity. Nobody is going to care. Because there, the official line will be that Pro killed Mick and his passenger."

Sam reached out and took Maria's hand. I knew he wanted to talk. Maybe she did too, or maybe she had come to terms with it all already.

"I know what you were both feeling. All you wanted was to be together and to be left in peace. But you had the immense, invincible power of Nelson's gang on the one side, and Mick and the law on the other. Your choices had all been taken away." I turned to Sam. "Your mother told me you were a real mensch, with a big pair of balls. I'd say she's right. What you did took real courage. You committed suicide, so that nobody would ever look for you again. Actually, you blew away one of Nelson's men. I should arrest you for that, but frankly I can't prove it and I don't care enough to try."

Maria was watching me, and there was real gratitude in her eyes. "And you—boy! You had the Triads, the Mob, the Sureños, and the NYPD all scratching their heads. But it was simple, really, wasn't it? You blew their minds. You had an apartment full of dope, and they all had you down as a submissive, obedient slave. How wrong they were. What did you do? Mix H in with their whiskey?

"I don't know if you had the shotgun there or if Sam took it over to you. I imagine it was already there as part of Nelson's arsenal. They were so damned stoned after you spiked their drinks, you could take your time and shoot each one of them, one after the other, at your leisure. Naturally, everybody assumed it was a hit squad who stormed in and had the job done in seconds. But it wasn't. It was you, taking your time.

"Some people break and go to pieces when you humiliate and abuse them. Others find a way to fight back. And that was you. And the message..." I turned to Dehan. "You said it was a message right from the start, remember? The message, when you castrated and beheaded him, was, 'this is a punishment killing. You try to dehumanize me, I will destroy you.'"

I heaved a big sigh and thought for a moment. "I am not sure if that was you or Sam. In a sense it was both of you. But I think Sam had gone directly to Texas. Because this was the real genius of your plan. Allow Mick to think that you were falling for him. He had told you that he was scamming the Triads and the Mob and that he had arranged for them to hit Nelson that night. You weren't even supposed to be there, were you? You were supposed to be at his place, waiting for him.

"How did it go? Mick and Pro were both screwing the Mob. They arranged to have the Mob and the Triads run into each other at Nelson's. Start a war between the gangs so the cops would assume the killing was part of gang warfare. Mick gets paid by the Mob straight into his account, and Pro collects his, in cash, from Nelson's apartment." I smiled and shook my head. "But when Pro turned up, his cash was gone. Because you had taken it."

She had that same impassive, expressionless look on her face. Sam's was the same. It was a technique they had mastered over the years, a way of dealing with what they had had to do in order to survive. I went on.

"Somewhere between New York and Shamrock you banked the money, because you had managed to persuade

Mick to give you the details of his numbered account. Was it Sam's idea to have two accounts? So if ever there was an investigation into Mick's crimes, it would stop at his unnumbered account, while the bulk of his money was in the numbered one?

"It struck me when the Feds found the account in Belize, that the amount of money in it was just enough to be convincing, but well below the estimates I'd heard of how much he had got away with." I paused. "Tell me about Shamrock."

She shrugged. "What's to tell? He thought he controlled the world. Really, he was so stupid he was like a puppet. I had arranged with Sam that we would meet at Shamrock. I told Mick I wanted to go out to eat, and he was naturally all for that. I kept making snide remarks about how the Irish were supposed to be big drinkers, but the people in this town just drank milk. I goaded him. When he started mouthing off and getting violent, I appealed to those nice people at the restaurant to call the sheriff."

"And while he was in the slammer," I said, "you hired a truck from old Ted. You left it near the Palo Duro Canyon, had Ted drive you back, and when Mick came out of jail with a huge hangover, you told him you wanted to get out of that place. You offered to drive, said you wanted to. Did you dope him?"

She nodded. "I had kept a dose of heroin and a syringe. I persuaded him to let me drive, and as we were heading out of town, I simply took the syringe from my bag. He had his eyes closed. I stuck him in the neck and rammed the plunger home. He convulsed. He would probably have died anyway from the overdose. But when we got to the site, I shot him in the belly with his own gun."

I said, "I hadn't noticed till I reviewed the case, after we got back from Texas, but of course you, Sam, were a medical student. It would have been easy for you to get hold of a woman's skull and a few bones. You met Maria at the site and left the bones in the car. You picked up the SUV you'd rented from Ted and headed out to start a new life in San Francisco."

Sam said, with some defiance in his voice, "What would you have done, Detective?"

I shrugged and stood. "It's irrelevant. You did what you did. The important thing, as far as I am concerned—" I turned to Dehan, who was watching me with her eyebrows arched. "—and I think Detective Dehan will agree, is that the criminals are all either dead or in custody, and you are free to care for your children and raise a good family."

Maria smiled, Sam frowned, and they both said simultaneously, "Thank you."

"I just ask one thing,"

Maria looked up at me. "What's that?"

Dehan answered for me. "Pick up the phone, Maria. Call your brother. He needs to be rescued. And call your mother, she misses you. That goes for you too, Sam."

Epilogue

WE WERE SITTING IN a place called the Epic Steakhouse, looking through the window at the Golden Gate Bridge. Dehan was sitting across the table from me getting intense about the best steak she had ever eaten in her life. I was wondering if I had died and gone to Valhalla. I was also wondering if I would have to mortgage my house to be able to pay for the wine. But if I did, I didn't mind. Things didn't get this good all that often in life.

She didn't look at me—she was too busy looking at her steak—but she stabbed her fork in my direction and said with her mouth full, "When did you realize it was Maria?"

I smacked my lips and leaned back.

"In the car, driving to Texas. I kept going over and over the same question. It had to be one of three people, but it wasn't either one of them. So it had to be that other, invisible person. That other person in the apartment was Maria. But how the hell could gentle, sweet Maria kill five guys with a shotgun before they even reached for their weapons? Then it dawned on me—they would be doped. And the apartment was full of dope. You know the old adage, poison is a woman's weapon. Once you accepted that, everything else just fell into place."

I chewed and sipped and smiled.

Dehan nodded quietly, then said, "So if Jennifer wasn't talking to Pro, who was—still is?"

"One of two people. We'll have to wait and see."

She grunted, then waved a steak knife at me and said, "You said that Maria was dead. But you knew she wasn't. You said Sam had killed her, but you knew he hadn't."

I sipped and smiled again.

"I was struggling with my conscience, Dehan. I trusted you implicitly. But it was not my secret to tell. It was theirs. So I spoke metaphorically and hoped that you would see the meaning of the metaphor. He, Sam, had killed her and himself so that they could be reborn in San Francisco. He's a smart guy." I gestured at her with my hand. "And you did get it, you being a subtle, intelligent, intense kind of person."

"Whatever. What you mean is you are vain and wanted to reveal it all at the end to show off."

"Perhaps. I have a certain..."

"Intellectual vanity. Yeah, I know."

"You followed me out to Frisco and stalked me."

"I knew you were holding out on me, and I knew you were going to get into trouble. I had to be there to bail you out." She smiled and winked.

I raised an eyebrow at her. "You were lucky I didn't nail you in the bedroom."

"Excuse me?"

"When you shot the guy Pro sent to kill me. I thought you were a second hit man."

"Oh." She chewed for a moment. Then said, "The way you were falling over yourself in the dark, I never felt I was in any danger of getting nailed by you."

"Thanks."

"So who was this psychoanalyst?"

I shook my head. "Just a very confused woman."

We smiled and raised our glasses. She said, "Cheers, Stone."

"Cheers, Dehan!"

And we drank deep.

NOTE FROM THE AUTHOR

IF YOU LIKED *ACE AND A PAIR* then please consider taking a second out of your day and leaving your thoughts behind for others.

It takes a couple seconds, but seriously would mean a ton to me and help get the word out there about my books!

Thanks,

Blake Banner

Made in the USA
Columbia, SC
17 July 2020